OVER THE MOON

g.g. eliot

To Becky and Lorna

First published in Great Britain in 2004
by Piccadilly Press Ltd.,
5 Castle Road, London NW1 8PR
www.piccadillypress.co.uk

A catalogue record for this book is available from the
British Library

ISBN: 1 85340 734 8 (trade paperback)

1 3 5 7 9 10 8 6 4 2

Printed and bound in Great Britain by Bookmarque Ltd
Typeset by Textype Typesetters
Cover design by Fielding Design
Set in 11/16 pt Goudy and GirlsAreWeird

Why Me?

'What exactly are you gawping at?'

I'm yelling at Kevin Small. He's one of our defenders. He's staring at me as if I'd just arrived from Never-Never-Land.

'Oh nothing, I just hadn't – er . . .'

'Hadn't – er – what?'

'Oh nothing.'

'No one stares at "oh nothing,"' I shout, 'not even you.'

By this time he's gone bright red. Just as I'm about to get further on his case, he turns and tears right up the pitch. Odd behaviour or what?

My name's Ella Christina Furgusson, I'm fourteen and I come from Rainsfield, just on the edge of London. I live in quite a nice old house with my big brother, Jamie (who I like lots) and my even bigger sister, Hannah (who I don't, much), my mum and dad, Christina and Roy (who are about as all right as it's fair to expect) and, oh yes, our psycho-pussy, Roger.

Anyway, my story starts, in case you hadn't guessed, on a football pitch – the one behind our leisure centre. I'm in goal. Does that sound weird – girly goalies and all that? It doesn't to me – I've always been into sports ever since I was a kid. I'm the only girl in our local team and, without showing off (which means I'm just about to), I'm quite good. This used to really piss off the others, but they couldn't find anyone else. Anyway, I save far more goals than I let in, so they soon got over it.

I'm quite tall, you see – about five-eight-and-a-bit last time I counted – and pretty fit. Not fit as in *fit* – to say that would be really big-headed (and untrue) – but fit as in running and jumping and leaping about and stuff. And . . . best of all, I don't have a problem getting really muddy. That's quite a big thing if you're in goal. Some of my mates at school think I'm on serious mad pills and take the mickey out of me all the time. They hate anything to do with mud and running about and outdoors. Mind you, most of them seem to hate anything that doesn't include the word 'boy'. Don't get me wrong, I do like boys – well, some boys – but with football and everything, they don't really seem to like me. Well, I suppose they like me, but they treat me as if I'm one of them.

So, where was I? Oh yes, it's right at the end of the game and I'm half freezing my bits off – hopping up and down to keep my hands and feet from going numb. It's two-one to us and there's about a minute to go. Victory looms, but bright-red-Kev has deserted his position – the creep – and I'm left all on my sad little ownsome in my big, cold, empty goal. Most of the play's been up at the other end of the pitch in the second half.

Suddenly one of their strikers, a tallish bloke with long blond hair (quite fit, actually) breaks through on the left and, having no one to challenge him, heads straight at me. Panic time or what? It's more or less an open goal with only yours truly in the way. I stretch my arms and legs to make myself as big as possible and offer up a quick prayer to the Lord above. When he's about twenty metres away (the other player – not the Lord above) he lets fly this awesome shot, at twice the speed of light, right at the corner of my goal. It's such a cracker, all I can do is fling myself to the side and up a bit, hoping I won't land on anything painful. I hardly see the flipping ball, but my prayers are answered. I don't know how. It's a complete fluke, but I just manage to get my left hand to it and it shoots over the bar (while I shoot into a puddle). Even our national keeper couldn't have out-goalied me. The ref blows his whistle and all our side and our six supporters go bonkers. Rainsfield Rangers (Junior League) have won. The rest of the lads run back cheering and carry the filthy but happy 'Hero(ine) of the Hour' – me – off the pitch shoulder-high. A good day's work I think.

When I'm in the shower and all alone, I start trying to get my head round what top deserter and prize starer Kevin was actually staring *at*. Then all of a sudden, like a flash, it comes to me and my own stupid face starts heating up too. Being tall and slim (most people call it skinny), I've been rather lacking in the old *breastular* department. Bee-stings, my sister calls them. But, just recently, they've started getting bigger and bigger. They're in no way what you'd actually call *big*, of course, but at least you can now see what side of the gender-fence I fall on when I take my top off. I exhausted my first bra in a few months. It's still languishing in my knicker drawer, having taken early retirement and now I'm ready for another one.

I stand in front of the mirror, check no one's coming, and then jig up and down again. Oh no! I mean, oh yeah, I can see exactly what carrot-top Kevin had his little piggy eyes on.

Even though I'm wearing a bra, my recent additions are jumping up and down like mad things. How completely and horribly embarrassing is that?

Kevin's obviously been singing their praises to the others, as, in the bus on the way home, the rest of the lads keep giggling and looking down when I try to talk to them. All except my brother Jamie, who seems well cross with them (oh yes – and his best mate Adam who doesn't seem to care either way). Jamie's cool and just a year older than me and has always protected me – but more about him (and Adam) when . . . when I get round to it.

Once we get indoors, I manage to get him to spill the beans.

'They're such a bunch of peanut-brains, that lot,' he says.

'Tell me something I don't know,' I say, 'but why now?' (As if I don't know.)

'You're not gonna like this, Ell, but I reckon it's the first time they've really sussed you're a girl. Sorry, but you know what I mean.'

I so *do* know what he means. I've hardly ever done any of the things girls normally do. My mum tells me that even when I was tiny I never had dolls or fluffy animals or any of that stuff (except a teddy called Guy who I ritually burned on bonfire night). I even asked for a tool set last Christmas. How girly's that?

'Thought so,' I say. 'I caught Kev staring at my boobs.'

'I know,' Jamie replies, looking all embarrassed, 'he was going on about them in the showers till I sorted him out with a wet towel on his fat red arse. It's funny, I suppose I've always thought of you as one of us too. It's because you fit in so well,

4

and with your short hair and everything, and your . . . well –
I, er . . .'

'Thanks a bunch. It's nice to find out you think I'm a boy.'

'Look Ella, don't get stroppy. It's just that you can do just
about everything us boys can do, and sometimes sort of
better. It used to piss me off.'

I nearly say thanks, but realise it isn't that much of a
compliment.

'Hey,' I say, 'you don't have a problem with me being in
the team, do you? You didn't say much at the time. Mind you,
knowing me, I most likely never asked.'

'No, of course not. I suppose we all thought it a bit weird
at first, especially when it got in the local paper, but I've
always thought it was quite cool having a footballing sister.
You know I can't stand really girly girls like you-know-who.'

We all know who 'you-know-who' is . . . my big sister
Hannah.

'I wouldn't mind seeing her playing footie in what she
usually wears,' I say, 'especially the black leather mini-skirt
and those high-heeled boots.'

I can't remember Hannah ever having done anything
vaguely sporty. All she does is go on about the blokes who
play sports. She doesn't exactly go for the pale, brainy types
(actually nor do I, to be totally truthful). From what I can
remember, she's already been out with two footie players,
three rugby players and a really thick tennis player with thick
legs and a flash car who nearly got into the last million or
something at Wimbledon.

5

Hannah doesn't exactly dislike me . . . it would almost be better if she did. Most times she acts as if she can't really see the point of my existence. Anyone who isn't into clothes, cars and Johnny Depp-lookalikes is a bit of a waste of space in her extremely thin book. I quite fancy Johnny Depp too, but I'd never tell *her* that. She treats everyone, including Jamie, who's only a year younger than her, like little people who aren't worth bothering with. But he won't take it, and calls her a dimbo-bimbo to her face. As for Mum and Dad, I'm pretty sure they know what she's like, but with them it's a parent thing.

Deep Thought for the Day

I feel sorry for parents sometimes. They sort of have to love you, it's their job. It must be in the instructions you get with a baby. Maybe even our form mistress, Miss Braithwaite's parents loved her once – or am I going too far?

Why Do I Have to Grow Up?

It's all a bit weird. I keep thinking about the boys and their stupid staring. When I get in from school on Monday, Mum immediately asks me what's wrong. It's funny how she always knows when I'm feeling crap.

'What's up, darling?'

'It's nothing really. It's just footie and all the boys there.'

'Why, what's happened, sweetie?'

'Oh you know . . .' I say, trailing off.

'Is there something wrong?' Mum asks, looking worried.

'All the boys in the team were giggling at my boobs. I just want to play footie, but they're so dumb. I don't know how long I'll be able to stay in the team – it's getting a bit much. I tried to talk to Beth* about it, but she seems to think it's no big deal. She doesn't really understand what I'm moaning about.'

'Oh darling, I'm sorry you're upset but you're growing up so fast, and the boys are growing up too. They're starting to notice the differences between you and them.'

'They're lucky – they don't have periods or boobs or bad hair days.'

'No, but they start getting hair sprouting everywhere and loads of spots and their voices change, and they become obsessed with their willies.'

'Is Jamie obsessed with his?'

---

*My best mate.

7

'Who knows? That's the other big problem with boys. They can't seem to talk about their feelings with anyone, not even their best mates.'

'Couldn't he talk to Dad?'

'*Especially* not Dad . . .'

'Why's that?'

'Oh, I don't know. Men just don't discuss that stuff – or anything to do with girlfriends, come to that. You probably know as much about your brother as me or your father.'

'The trouble is, Mum, I'm really happy as I am – honest. It's everyone else who's changing. Even Beth's started rabbiting on about boys and sex all the time.'

'Well, you don't seem to mind boys. I've seen all the pictures in your room.'

'Oh, you mean Will Bradley! He's got a great voice – all sort of gravelly. I really like *him*, but I don't think much of the boys at school, or the ones in the team. They're just mates. At least as far as I'm concerned.'

'But they're beginning to see you as a girl. That's the trouble.'

'But I'm all gawky and I've got braces on my teeth and that. They call me tin-grin!'

'Yes, but you won't have them much longer – aren't they due to come out in a couple of weeks?'

'When do you think my boobs'll stop growing? I'll look like one of those girls on the top shelf of the newsagents if I'm not careful. How rank is that?'

'When I was your age all my friends wanted to look like that! Just be happy that they're growing at all, and try not to worry too much. Anyway, don't rush into anything until you feel ready. You've tons of time.'

'Thanks, Ma. By the way, I think I'll have to have another bra. This one's starting to cut into my back. Either it's shrinking or I'm growing. If everyone was like me, they'd have to put the factory on overtime.'

'Do you want me to come with you?'

'Would you, Mum? I still get a bit – well, you know . . .'

'I was just the same at your age.'

I bet she wasn't!

Hannah, Adam and Playing Footie

'Ella . . . are you up there? It's your playmates come to collect you.'

It's my sister Hannah calling from downstairs. She always calls the blokes I play football with 'my playmates'. It's her way of winding me up and putting me down at the same time. It's soooooo funny – not!

At seventeen my sister's OK – quite pretty really, in a rather obvious sort of way. Far too in-your-face for my liking. The real drag is, like I said before, she always treats me like I'm a little kid and has done since I actually was one. She still goes to my school, but won't stay much longer if she gets her way. Mum and Dad want her to go on to uni because, underneath it all, they think she's quite clever, but she never did do studying.

Hannah's one of those people who spends more time worrying about what she looks like than anything else – oh yeah, that, and boys of course. I suppose that follows. If I had a quid for each time she's said 'he said this', or 'he said that', or 'he's always trying to get me to do this' – I'd never have to work when I leave school. Tedious or what? Oh yes, and with the amount she's on her mobile, the lump of grey doughy stuff that used to be her brain must be well and truly fried by now. No great loss to the intellectual future of Britain, though.

Deep Thought for the Day

What did people do before mobile phones? Beth and I text each other practically every time we do anything. I reckon that eventually it'll get to a point where, when people meet, they'll just stand gawping, because they've covered everything already on the phone. You'll have restaurants full of couples not talking to each other but gabbling away to their mates who aren't there, filling them in on what's not been happening!

'Ella, are you coming down or not? I'm wearing my voice out.'

'Yeah, coming,' I yell back. 'Tell them to hang on a mo.'

I get to the bottom of the stairs where she's still waiting. Why exactly *is* she waiting? What now?

'You know that boy Adam Cresswell, who's out there with the others?'

'Yeah – course,' I say, beginning already to wonder where this is heading.

'He's got a brother called Gregory.'

'I should think he might know that,' I answer rather clever-dickily. 'So what?'

'Well, he has, hasn't he?'

'I think so.'

Think so? I so know so. Adam's brother 'Gorgeous Greg' (as we call him), is on every girl's must-snog list. He's top of our class 'Fit List' at school as well – over footballers, musicians and movie stars. He's about six feet tall, really fit, and according to anyone who's had the pleasure, dead cool. He's apparently going to Cambridge to do a degree in Extreme Cleverness.

11

'Do you ever see him when you go round to your little friend's house?' she asks.

'Look, Adam's not my little friend, thank you ever so much. He's the same age as Jamie, and taller than you . . . and no, I've never been to his house – not yet. What's that got to do with you, anyway?'

'Oh, nothing. It's just if you were ever over there and needed a lift back, I'd be only too happy to oblige.'

Hannah's just passed her driving test (God help all motorists and lollipop ladies!) and seems to drive Mum's Clio more than Mum does.

'How subtle is that?' I reply. 'Anyway, since when have you ever wanted to do me a favour?'

Hannah's not an idiot. Stupid sometimes . . . but not an idiot. She realises she went in a bit too obvious-like and tries to save face.

'Oh, go away and play your football. See if I care. You wouldn't understand anyway, being half boy.'

I actually understand quite well, but can't be bothered. Outside, Adam, Kevin, Dean and Gary are waiting. My brother Jamie's already down at the pitch with the rest of them.

'Hi, Ell,' says Gary. 'Are you up for a kick around?'

'Sure thing. I'll go and slip into something more sporty.'

I'm just wearing my slobbing-around-the-house clothes at the moment – a pair of woolly tracksuit bottoms and a short T-shirt (and more importantly no bra!).

'Shall we come and help?' he asks in a really cheeky voice.

I glare at Gary, hardly believing I heard right. He's staring at my front, probably regretting he said it. Oh no, here we go again. I can feel myself going red. I know exactly what he's on about, but I know I've got to hold my own with that lot or I'm sunk. It's all a bit weird, no one's ever hit on me like this before.

'Sorry, I don't have the foggiest what you're talking about. Do you mean help me put my trainers on? You must be mad.'

The boys all look like they've just got off a bus from Sniggersville-on-Sea, so I put the boot in a bit harder – after all, a girl's gotta do what a girl's gotta do if she's to survive in this cruel world.

'If you lot really want to help me change, come on in,' I say, knowing full well that it'll send them running the other way.

Brill! Beat them at their own game, the weirdos. They all look round as if daring each other and then start chucking the ball around as if they haven't heard. Talk about chicken!

As for the subject of their comments (my boobs); after that little episode last Saturday, I went into town after school with Mum and bought not only a new bra, but a special one for sports. Not *très* sexy, I admit – but I can't have my bouncy friends knocking me about or showing off, can I? And I can't have the whole team staring at them every time I feel the urge to jig up and down. Now, I reckon, I could carry around two extra-wobbly pink jellies without anyone noticing.

When I'm back upstairs, I squint through the side bit of the blinds and do some amateur boy-spotting from my room. They're all out in the street pushing each other around and giggling – probably at what Gary said. I don't suppose I've ever really studied them before as potential boyfriend material (I've never studied anyone much as potential boyfriend material, come to that), they've just been the guys I play footie with. Kevin Small's out for a start – too podgy, too childish and too ginger. Height-wise, Dean Williams is a bit of a toddler – vertically challenged, as they say. Quite nice-looking in the facial department, I suppose, but a lot shorter than me. He'd need to stand on a box to snog me (or I'd need to stand in a hole). Gary Scott's not bad either, but he's a bit skinny (who am I calling skinny?) and has just started cultivating an urban spot farm on his face. It would be like snogging a minefield. That leaves Adam Cresswell. I home in on Adam and suddenly realise he's quite cool-looking, eight out of ten even. He's got slightly gingery hair and the trillion freckles that go with it – cut really short and sticky-uppy, but he has a slim, fit body and a great wide smile with ever such white teeth. Best of all, he's the same height as me. Yeah, Adam, compared to the rest of the human race, is not that awful at all . . . for a boy! Trouble is, he's the only one who doesn't seem to be the least bit interested in me. He never sniggers like the rest of them. I must admit to myself that I do sort of fancy him (sort of), but for all I know, he could think I'm just one of the boys, like my brother.

Another Deep Thought for the Day

Funny, isn't it? If someone who you don't fancy stares at you, it's a real turn-off, but if it's someone you do quite fancy, they're just taking a healthy interest. There's no answer to that.

I check myself in the mirror. Yuck! I really am not the fairest in the land at the moment. Must do something about my hair. I look like I should work in a library or a petrol station or a prison, even. I keep it shortish for all the sport I do – running about and jumping and stuff, but it really does me no favours looks-wise. Then there's the Full Metal Brace I wear to do battle with my goofy teeth. It's coming out soon – thank the Lord. I've forgotten what my teeth look like. Apart from all that, I reckon my head's a bit on the small side. Miss Leonardo da Jenkins, the old fart who takes us for art, says that when you draw people, the head should go into the body seven times. Mine goes in about twenty, I reckon. Mind you if it was down to volume not height, her head would go into her body about two hundred. No, if I grew my hair long, I wouldn't look like such a pin-head. On the other hand, those really slinky fashion models have got the same sort of set up as me . . . and most of them are seriously underdeveloped in the boob department, which it now looks as if I won't be – thanks to Mother Nature. I hope they don't get too big, though, or I'll look like a snake that's swallowed a couple of rats side-by-side.

On the way to the park I end up, accidentally-on-purpose, talking to Adam.

'You know that goal you saved last Saturday,' he says.

'Yeah! How could I forget it?'

'The ref was blind. It wouldn't have been allowed anyway.'

'Course it would. Why wouldn't it have been?'

'Because that bloke from the other team was offside. It was obvious.'

'No, he wasn't!' I come back snappily. 'He broke through right from the other end of the pitch. Both our defenders were off playing silly buggers.'

'It doesn't matter anyway. Look, I wasn't trying to put you down. But he was between them and our goal when the ball was passed to him.'

'So? He still brought it all the way up to me.'

'I know. I didn't say that to piss you off – it was a great save.'

'What you're saying is, I needn't have bothered. Oh well, you must educate me, oh master. I am only a mere girlie, after all. What do I know of such things?'

'I didn't mean it like that, honest. I think you're really good.'

'Yeah, but I'd be much better if I understood the rules though, eh? Thanks a bunch.'

'Look, I . . .'

At that moment we pass through the gates and Kevin hoofs the ball over to Adam. Adam looks at me all sort of cross and hurt at the same time, and then gallops off to join the others.

'Well done, Ell!' I say to myself. 'I think you just might have blown that particular love affair for ever and ever.'

I stop walking and try to remember what he said to me – the exact words. Didn't he say he thought I was good? Yes, I'm sure he did. I'm sure he didn't just say good at football. But who am I kidding? He only meant in goal – not good as a person, worse luck. Not that it matters now, seeing as I've gone and pissed him off big time. Oh well Ell, it's beginning to look as if once I even get a look at someone I quite fancy, big old metal-mouth will muck it up good and proper. I guess I really need a bit more practice. This fancying business is all a bit new.

I run into the park and start kicking the ball around for a bit with the others. But something's different and I can't quite get my head round it. I might be wrong, but the lads don't seem to be tackling or kicking so hard when I'm around, like they're giving me a chance. I start to wonder if it's because they've really taken in that I'm a girl. Weirdest of all, they're all being dead nice to me – not taking the piss as usual.

Suddenly, one of the balls hits me right in the chest and Sean Peacock, I think it was, comes over and says sorry. *Sorry?*

Who ever says sorry on a football pitch? And to a goalie? Come to that, who ever says anything nice on a football pitch? (Unless you score, that is!) I mean, you can just see Mr Beckham apologising for hitting some enemy keeper when he'd just got in the way of his penalty shot, can't you? 'Excuse me, terribly sorry, I won't kick it so hard next time – promise!'

Then I notice something else. Every time I get into a tangle in goal, I keep feeling hands brushing against by boobs . . . and then the penny drops – duh! Apart from Jamie and Adam, they all seem to be playing that stupid game I heard about at school. My best mate Beth and I were talking about it last week. Boys do this thing where they score points for touching various girls' bits. One for an arm, two for a leg, three for a bum and about ten for a boob. They just touch us subtly in the corridor or the lunch queue. The secret's not to be noticed, apparently. Juvenile or what?

Anyone Seen Argentina?

'Ell – it's me.'

'Me' usually means Beth – Beth Middleton. She's on her mobile. Normally we just text because phoning is too expensive. Beth's short for Elizabeth, by the way, so you can see why she changed it. We reckon Elizabeth sounds a bit like a vicar's wife or a head teacher (or a queen, even!). I've been lying on the bed thinking about my ex-potential boyfriend, Adam Cresswell. I wonder what he's doing at this very moment in time. You can bet next month's allowance he's not thinking about me.

'Hi sweet, how you diddlin'?' I say.

'Oh, *pas mal, mon amie, merci beaucoup*. Can't get my head round my geography homework though. Where's Argentina this week?'

'Search me. I can't even find my geography homework.'

'Jeez, you really are worse than me. Can I come round?'

'Course. We can go geog-ing together. Could you bring Argentina with you?'

Beth's brilliant. She's the coolest person I know by far – and the brightest. In all the time I've known her, which is nearly all my life, I can't ever remember having a really big argument. We shout and scream and stuff and take the piss (who doesn't?) but we always end up falling about giggling. If we do argue, it's mostly about really mind-blowingly important things like who we fancy and who's going to do what to who in the soaps. I think she looks *gorgeous*, but she's always going on about her weight. She says she looks like a human hippo, but I usually say things like, that's unfair to hippos, and for some reason it makes it better (that's after she's whacked me). We're a bit of a weird pair, us two – me all gawky and sharp corners with a full metal-mouth and her all soft and voluptuous and pretty . . . Beauty and the Stick – that's us. Beth never had to wait for her first bra delivery either – she was practically born with boobs. That's probably why she went a bit off when mine turned up – like it wasn't fair kind of thing – like skinny people with long legs shouldn't be issued with them.

Deep Thought for the Day
Aren't breasts weird? You spend so much time in life worrying if you're ever going to get any, then you spend the rest of the time covering them up and making sure they don't wobble or make a spectacle of themselves.

Back to Beth. She finds it difficult being from a mixed-race background. Her dad, Henry, is black and is very good-looking. He mends hearts in a big hospital and is quite loaded. They live in a big house and he drives something smart and shiny and German. Beth's dad is quite a laugh (for a grown-up). Beth's mum is called Sandra and she's white and lovely and round and cuddly. Beth says she feels she's not one thing nor the other and different from the rest of us.

'Ella, it's Beth. Can she come up?' my mother calls from downstairs.

'Sure, Ma,' I yell back.

19

'Hi babe, did you find it?' I ask as Beth walks in.

'What – your room? Oh, you know – same way as usual. Top of the stairs, turn right . . .'

'No, you dork. Argentina.'

'Oh, that. I'd splashed some hot chocolate over the word when I was looking at the map. It wasn't where I thought. It's the thick bit on the right of Chile.'

'OK smart-arse, so where's Chile?'

'Left of Argentina, silly. It's stuck on the bottom of South America somewhere.'

For me, finding where a country is in geography is a bit like that stupid game where you wear a blindfold and try to pin the tail on a drawing of a donkey. We used to play that at my nursery school Christmas party when I was little. We thought it was funny then.

'Nobody told me,' I continue. 'Anyway, what have we got to do?'

'Oh, not much – just do a map with all the main features.'

'What? Like llamas and stuff?'

'No, idiot, we've got to put in all the mountains and rivers and cities.'

'What? No llamas?' I say.

Beth looks at me strangely.

'I do seriously hope you're joking, Miss Furgusson.'

'I guess this puts exploring out as a living,' I say mock-mournfully. The only sort of exploring I'd do is round places where there was nothing hurty or bitey.

'You wouldn't even find the map,' Beth says wearily.

'Are you coming down the leisure centre on Friday?' I ask, changing gear clumsily.

'You playing football?'

'Yeah, but we're all going for an *après*-footie pizza.'

'And Jamie?' (Beth really fancies my brother, but never really admits to it.)

'Yeah, course – he's just been made captain.'

'Cool! You're so lucky to be part of that lot.'

'I bet you could be too.'

'Oh yeah – what as . . . the ball?'

'Now stop that! Don't be soft.'

'They'd only have to put me in goal and I'd be the perfect keeper! Nothing could ever get past.'

'Look, shut it,' I say, almost crossly.

'You've no idea what it's like for me! I'm just about to start my millionth diet.'

'Which one now?'

'I'm going to have a go at that one people are always going on about – that high protein, high fat, low carbohydrate one. I got the book out of the library.'

'Is that the library where I saw all those fat people going in and thin people coming out?' I can't help laughing at my own joke.

'Very funny,' says Beth, trying her hardest to keep a straight face.

'Seriously, what's so different? Aren't they all the same? One cornflake for brekkie, half a lettuce leaf for lunch and a sandwich for tea – with no bread.'

'This one's cool. It says you can eat all the things the others tell you not to. All the things with lots of fat in – like meat and eggs and bacon and cheese and stuff.'

'I reckon that's bonkers.'

'The bloke who wrote the book says that it's all the other things that make you fat.'

'Like?'

'Like brown bread, muesli, rice, juice and fruit and stuff. Everything you don't want, anyway.'

'Is this author bloke thin?'

'I expect so now – he died a few years ago. He was really rich, though – he sold millions of books.'

'Didn't help him though, did it?'

'It was an accident, he tripped over and banged his head, apparently.'

'Probably tripped over a pile of money. So, do they reckon it really works?'

'Apparently. I don't dare tell my dad, though. He'd go through the roof.'

'Why?'

'According to him, all the things this bloke says you should go for, are the ones that make your heart stop going. They all make cholesterol, he says.'

'Is that what clogs up your arteries?'

'Apparently. Mind you, I don't care. I'd try anything if it'd make me thin and ever so desirable.'

'You get very thin when you're dead, I've heard – and sorry, but dead women are not particularly desirable – especially to men. Well, most men!'

'Yeah, but there must be a bit before you die when you're just right.'

'Beth! Have you caught a double dose of mad cow disease? You're just right as you are. It's probably in your genes.'

'You're kidding, aren't you? I can hardly get into them.'

'Don't be silly. I used to dream of looking like you.'

'Used to, yeah. Before you realised slim is beautiful.'

'Maybe we should combine ourselves, you know, take the best bits of both of us. Couldn't your dad do that? He's in the cutting-up-people-and-putting-them-back-together business, isn't he?'

'Oh yeah, Ell. I could just see his face if I asked him tonight if he knows anyone who could mix me and you together. He'd go white.'

'It'd be great – I'd have permanent suntan.'

'Knowing my luck, we'd end up tall and fat and metal teeth,' says Beth.

'And stripy.'

We both tumble on to the bed, giggling at the thought.

Another Deep Thought for the Day

The world's such a crazy place. Half the population's desperately trying to find enough food to keep themselves alive, while the other half stuff their faces with all the food that should be shared around . . . and then they spend a fortune on diets to stop themselves dying from obesity. It's a shame we can't feed the very fat ones to the very thin ones, I say.

Enter Miss Braithwaite

Beth and I get to school a bit early the following morning. Two of our friends, Zoe Danvers and Charlie Simpson are hanging around in the loos waiting for the bell to ring because it's raining. Charlie's just gone blond and we're all admiring it.

'It makes you look like someone else,' says Beth. 'Didn't your mum and dad mind?'

'Mum helped me do it. She does hers with the same stuff. I think it's wicked.'

'What do you think old Miss B will say?' I ask.

'She can say what she bloody well wants. There aren't any anti-blond rules, are there?'

'I bet if I did anything like that, she'd be on my case immediately,' I say.

'Have you ever thought of doing yours, Ell?' asks Zoe, who's got long natural blond hair (creep!).

'I can't be bothered. I once thought I could have it done the same as our football shirts.'

'What? Green and mauve? That'd be lush,' says Beth, who always was a bit peculiar.

Zoe then turns to me again.

'Is it true? Beth was telling us the boys in your team started feeling you up.'

'Yeah, I was really pissed off.'

'That sounds a better reason for playing than any other I've heard,' says Charlie.

Charlie has a bit of a reputation for being not the most difficult person in the whole universe to get off with.

'Rugby would be better,' says Beth with a giggle. 'I could do some real damage in the scrum. I'd be the one right in the middle.'

'Look, why can't I just play football, without having my boobs felt every five minutes?'

'You're lucky to have any,' says Zoe sadly. She still suffers from boobular deprivation (that's a condition that Beth and I have made up).

'Ah, Ella Furgusson, so glad to see you. I was beginning to wonder whether you were still residing on our planet.'

We're now in class and Miss Braithwaite, our form mistress and geography teacher (a pain in the butt and frightfully posh), is on my case already. I think she must've been marking my homework. I'm staring out of the window thinking about you-know-who, when she settles on me like a starving wasp on a jam pot.

'Er, yes Miss Braithwaite,' I reply, 'Cranleigh Drive – number thirty-one.'

Nervous giggles from around class. Miss B ignores them.

'It would appear that Argentina, on your rather bizarre version of planet Earth, is not much larger than Wales. Seeing as the country has a population of nearly thirty-five million, I'm sure they would not fully appreciate what you've done to their land. Might I ask where you intend to put them all?'

'I'm afraid I couldn't get it all in, Miss,' I say brightly.

More giggles from around the class, especially from Donna who sounds a bit like a horse when she laughs and usually sets everyone else off.

'I'm afraid when map-making, Ella, the cartographer doesn't often enjoy the luxury of altering the size of whole countries in order that they might, as you so eloquently put it, fit in. The only person with the power to do that sort of thing is our Creator. Isn't that right, Emma?'

She knows Emma's dad's a vicar and for some reason thinks that Emma must be full of deep religiousness. If only she knew! Miss Braithwaite also takes us for RE, in case you wondered why she'd said such a naff thing. Silly old cow, she loves going on like this and making you look stupid.

'He wasn't around when I was doing my homework, Miss,' said Emma.

Miss B tries her hardest to look angry, but try as she might, she can't avoid a slight smiley twitch as the rest of the class falls about. When the noise dies down she goes off again.

'Ella Furgusson! Much as we all appreciate your role as class jester, you will soon be approaching your GCSEs. While your classmates might be able to see the humorous side of your appalling ignorance, I'm sure the examining board won't. You will do the map again in your own time.'

I scowl at Beth on the far side of the class (we were forcibly separated about three days into the first term). Beth beams across, as if to say, 'That'll teach you to listen to me.' It turns out she'd realised and altered hers before handing it in. How sneaky is that?

Actually, I usually do all right at school (more than all

right sometimes), but geography bores me so stiff I can hardly move. I mean, I don't have a problem with 'abroad' when I go there, but all that population and rainfall and rivers and deltas and stuff leaves me cold.

Just as we're escaping to first break, Beth and I spot a new notice on the school notice-board.

Beth reads it out loud:

'There is to be a Grand Valentine's Ball in the town hall on Saturday 14th February. The proceeds will go towards the proposed refurbishment of the Rainsfield Leisure Centre. Dress will be black tie. Tickets, to include a glass of champagne and a buffet supper, will be twenty-five pounds.'

'Sounds naff,' I say. 'Catch me in a big frock? Anyway, I bet it's only for sixth-formers. They'd never give us a glass of champagne.'

'Hang on,' says Beth, 'I didn't finish. It says here that the music will include The Fugitives, with the Will Bradley Band heading the bill. Do you see that, Ell? I'm not imagining it, am I? The Will Bradley Band – look there.'

'Who'd have thought he'd come here! That's mega-cool. They must be paying a bloody fortune, or he's doing it on the cheap. Hang on, I think I remember someone telling me he comes from round here. Perhaps he's coming back to his roots. We can't miss him, Beth.'

'No way! So where are we going to get twenty-five squidlies, Miss Almighty Moneybags? There isn't a Help the Potless Schoolgirls charity that I've ever heard of. I don't know about you, but I've spent all my Christmas money. And what are you going to wear – your football strip?'

'You're so not hearing me, doh. I said we *can't* miss it. C . . . a . . . n . . . t! We'd never live with ourselves knowing *he'd* been to Rainsfield, never mind The Fugitives.'

'But twenty-five quid? And then we've got to get hold of the clothes and all that. And that's if we can persuade our mums and dads to let us go. Have you thought of that little problemo?'

'Leave it to me. Where there's a will there's a way . . . or should I say, where there's a Will Bradley there's a way.'

I look up the corridor only to see my sister, Hannah, with a couple of her mates coming towards us. 'Oh sh-ugar, here comes Han. She's seen us.'

'What are you two gawping at? Not the poster for the ball, I hope? I'm afraid it's not really suitable for you lot. No jellies or conjurors involved.'

Her two mates cackle like witches. Hannah loves to show off.

'We'll need a bloody conjuror to get us in,' murmurs Beth.

'What's that?' says Hannah.

'Oh nothing, we don't want to go anyway. Sounds far too stuck-up.'

'I thought you had the hots for Will Bradley, Ella?'

'He's all right,' I lie.

In the world of mere mortals, Will Bradley's somewhere else. He's only the same height as me, but dead sexy, and sounds really mean . . . and he plays the guitar better than just about anyone I've ever clapped ears on. I'd just die a loathsome, lingering death if I missed him (and think how upset *he'd* be!).

All through English literature I'm in a bit of a trance, not

28

helped by trying to get my head round Chaucer. He wrote *Canterbury Tales* about these weird religious blokes going on holiday to Canterbury and telling stories on the way.

Trouble is, I just can't get the forthcoming ball out of my mind. How on earth am I, who owe my parents for just about everything (including my last two mobe bills plus a bit of Christmas present debt), going to diddle them or anyone else out of twenty-five squids plus?

During lunch break I run across my brother Jamie and decide to let him in on it.

'It sounds like just about everything I wouldn't be seen dead at,' he says. 'I really don't do smart, but I suppose I can understand wanting to see the Will Bradley Band – they're wicked. Does Beth want to go?'

'Yeah, as much as me. Why, does that make a difference?'

'No. Why should it? It just sounds like it could be a bit more of a laugh than it did at first.'

'Gee, thanks. Listen, do you fancy Beth, Jamie?'

Jamie stares at me and his mouth falls open. It's like the question that must never be asked – like how big's your willy?

'Leave it out, Ell.'

'Hmm! Unsatisfactory answer, I'm afraid. I suppose I'll have to let you off with a warning. Now, can you think of a way of getting hold of that sort of dosh?'

'I suppose bank robbery or international drug dealing is out of the question?'

'Blimey Jamie, we only need fifty quid!'

'I know, but it sounds a lot when you haven't got the price of a bag of chips.'

'Tell me about it. Then we'll need some sort of dress and proper shoes and all that nonsense.'

'I thought you hated dressing up.'

'I do, but Will Bradley's going to be there. I can't go to a ball in jeans, can I? Don't worry, mate, I'm not going to make a habit of it.'

'What about selling our bodies to medical science?' Jamie suggests.

'Very clever, not only are they not worth that much, but we'd hardly be able to go to a ball if we've got a load of bits missing.'

Jamie then goes silent for a while, as if he's remembering something.

'Hang on, I *have* got an idea. Did you go to that boot sale we did for the club last year?'

'Yeah, it was a bit of a wash-out, wasn't it? Didn't it pee down all day?'

'Yeah, but we still made over two hundred and fifty quid.'

'What? With all that rubbish?'

'Yeah, and that was after expenses.'

'You're pulling my leg!' I say. 'Blimey, do you reckon we could do that – me and Beth?'

'Can't see why not. Do you reckon you could get enough stuff together?'

'That'd be the easiest bit. Do you remember Gran saying that she's going to have to throw out practically everything from her house when she moves into her new place?'

'Wow! You're right. Some of it's quite good stuff – if you like that kind of thing.'

'I've got shed-loads of junk of my own that I don't want any more and there's a great big box of Hannah's Cindy dolls in the garage.'

'You could have all my Action Men too.'

'If we put them all in the same box now, we could have thousands by the time we do the sale!'

(I worry about myself sometimes.)

'What, like rabbits?' Jamie says, laughing. 'I don't know if my Action Men are up to it. I think half of them are gay anyway. I tell you what, though, it would make a bloody good movie – better than *Toy Story*. Look Ell, if I help you, will you cut me in on it? I could really use some money. I could get all the guys in the football team to ask their parents for anything they don't need.'

'But where could we do it?'

'Do you think Mum and Dad would let us have a sale in our front garden?' Jamie asks with a big frown.

'I reckon they'd rejoice at the idea of getting rid of some of my things. I think I'd have more trouble persuading them to let me go to the ball.'

'You're not wrong. What do you think they'll say?'

'Quite a lot, seeing as they still think I'm about ten.'

'I know what you mean. I keep telling them you're growing up.'

'I'm sure Hannah will be there. She'll probably get some bloke to take her.'

'Yeah, and then dump him if she sees something better inside.'

'I don't know why they put up with it.'

'I think I do – she looks pretty good until you get to know her.'

I love my big brother. He's such a mint geezer (I heard someone say that on telly).

Deep Thought for the Day

Aren't boot sales crackers? They're usually full of all the things that families have never used or even looked at. All those crap gifty things you get given by rellies when they've been on their hols, or birthday presents that you never wanted, or gadgets your mum bought that never really worked – like those awful sandwich-toasters that make the whole house stink. I reckon they'll be sold on again a couple of months later by the same people who bought them. It's like continuous recycling.

You Shall Go to the Ball

I have to ring Beth and let her in on the great plan.

'Hi Beth . . . Ella Christina Furgusson here, the most geniustical humanoid in the whole universe.'

'Hang on, I thought that was me! Anyway, why's that, O great one?'

'Oh, nothing much. It's just that I've come up with a dead easy way to make a large amount of loot quick.'

'I hope you're not going to sell your body.'

'Ha bloody ha. That's what Jamie said.'

'Anyway, who'd have it?' she asks.

'You may laugh, Miss Never-go-anywhere-never-do-anything. You just carry on being poor and stuck indoors. I'll tell you what life's like after I've done it all. I'm bound to meet the most gorgeous bloke at the ball and be dragged off to a tropical island in his private jet for who knows what.'

'Sorry – did that last week. I left him there all exhausted. All right, clever pants, I give in. Let's have it. How are we going to make all this cash, eh?'

'Actually, I lied – it was Jamie's idea.'

'Aha, suddenly I'm all ears,' Beth says, giggling.

'You're such a creepy creepster! I bet you'll think it's absolutely fantabuloso because he thought of it. He suggested we did a boot sale, or in our case a lawn sale – as we haven't got a boot.'

'What, in your front garden – like they do in America?'

'No, stupid, at Buckingham Palace! Of course in our front garden.'

'Oh yeah, and with what – our old school knickers and a herd of My Little Bald Ponies?'

(Beth cut all the manes and tails off hers in a fit of rage one day when she was little.)

'O ye of little faith. Me and Jamie reckon that we could fill a garage with all the junk from our family alone. I bet your parents have got heaps of stuff they don't need.'

'Yeah, like me at the moment. I just asked Mum if I could go to the ball and she went bal-bloody-listic. Like your sister said, she'd only let me go if there were balloons on the front door, lemonade, a conjuror . . . and a goody-bag to take home.'

'I haven't even asked mine yet. Look, I've got an idea. Mum and Dad think the sun shines out of Jamie's bum at the mo. If they knew he was coming they might think about it. He could be our chaper . . . what's that word?'

'Chaperone. Jeez, Ell, I reckon even *my* mum might go for that. For some bizarre and misinformed reason she thinks that your family are sensible and responsible.'

'What about your dad? I thought he was quite strict.'

'Oh, he's like most dads; he just does what Mum tells him – or else. Do you think Jamie'll go for it?'

'Absolutely. He likes the bands as well. And . . . I almost forgot. Guess what?'

'What?'

'He asked if you were going. At first he couldn't be bothered until I said you were.'

'You what?'

'When I told him you were going, he changed his mind big time.'

'Are you telling porcupines again?'

'No, promise. Then I asked him straight out if he fancied you.'

'You didn't! Oh no! You didn't . . . oh, hell! Ella! You bloody didn't . . . *did you?*'

'I thought you wanted to know,' I say with a little smile to myself.

'What did he say? I'll kill you for this, Ella. I'll kill you to death.'

'He smiled a sort of knowing smile – you know, like he does. Anyway, I'm the last person he'd tell.'

'See! That means he doesn't, doesn't it?'

'You silly moo, it means nothing of the sort. In my book it means he probably does.'

'Oh damn and blast! Jeez, what am I going to do? I won't be able to talk to him or anything ever again. This is so awful, I could die.'

'Are you are totally and completely off your trolley? One minute you can't get my brother off your feeble excuse for a mind, the next you're pulling your hair out, because he might fancy you.'

'That's *so* not the point.'

'Oh yeah, so what *so* is?'

'The point is, I don't know how to handle it any more.'

'Look, Beth, as your elder by three weeks and wiser by seven hundred years – mate, just take my advice. Play it dead cool, man. You don't want to frighten him off. Just pretend you've heard nothing and act your normal stupid self.'

'Oh hell, Ell, we'd better get this sale thingy under way pretty damn smart. There's no way I'm *not* going to that flipping ball now. I'd better double-up the circuit training.'

'Hang on a moment, Beth, darling friend. Do I detect an incy-wincy bit more enthusiasm for the sale now, or is it my vivid imagination?'

'All right, stop taking the mick. You win. You're not wrong. I think it's about the only way we stand a chance of raising the money. Now stop yabbering and let's make some plans.'

'It could be a real laugh. I've never tried to raise money before.'

'I should do a sponsored weight-loss. That's the only way I'm going to manage to lose any. Quid a pound.'

'Don't be daft. Nobody's got that much money – sorry! Anyway you don't want to get too thin, do you?'

'I hope that was a joke, too. The day I become too thin, all the world's chocolate factories will have finally closed down.'

'What about your diet?'

'I'm still doing it, but I'm going to try exercise alongside it.'

'You should join me at footie practice,' I say.

'Aren't you playing on Saturday?'

'Yeah, it's a biggie. We're playing Bourne End Rovers. They're top of the league.'

'By the way, do the others still touch you up?'

'They didn't at practice. Maybe they're settling down a bit.'

'Shame!'

'Beth, you're such a perv.'

'Only taking a healthy interest.'

Parties I Have Missed

It's raining, it's Monday morning, we lost badly on Saturday (I was crap), so I'm grumpy and I'm walking down Lawrence Avenue on the way to school (worse luck) and wondering, if I just happen to pass Adam Cresswell's road, which is way out of my way by about three hundred miles, whether I might accidentally-on-purpose run into him. I've still got to make things up. God knows what I'll say.

Instead, I run into Rachel Hunt and Becky Swithin. Being the moody cowlet that I sometimes am, there are times I don't really want to walk or talk with anyone (except Adam maybe) – and this is one of those times – but they're in my class so I sort of have to. It's a bit like when you meet neighbours in the street. You've got less than nothing to say, but it's polite. Anyway, Rache and Becks are yapping away at a hundred miles per hour about Emma's fifteenth birthday party last weekend.

Deep Thought for the Day
I sometimes think people enjoy talking about something they did more than they actually enjoyed doing it.

'Did you snog Darren after we cleared off?' asks Rache (bit of a goer but quite nice). 'It looked like it was heading that way.'

'I thought it was never going to happen,' says Becks (a mega-mouth, but dead funny sometimes). 'Talk about slow. I

eventually had to drag him into the back garden. Not bad –
a bit frantic though when he got going – and he kept trying
to get his hand in my top.'

'Did you let him?'

'For about two seconds, then we had to stop.'

'Why?'

'Because my dad turned up.'

'They should invent a father alarm,' I say brightly, but the
joke goes down in flames.

'Sarah said he was at the front door,' she went on, hardly
stopping to breathe. 'It was a good job he didn't come round
the side of the house. He nearly did he said. There was so
much racket apparently, no one heard the door for ages.'

'Saved by the bell, eh?' I try again.

'How did you get on?' Rache continues, ignoring my
comment. 'Didn't I see you wrapped round Jake Whitfield?'

'That was just for starters. I moved on from there. I ended
up with Billy Dawson.'

'*Billy Dawson?* Are you bonkers? He's a sex maniac, yeah,
and rank with it. Weren't Emma's parents around? They're
usually in and out of the bedrooms every five minutes.'

'With buckets of cold water,' I throw in.

The other two stop and stare like I'm from Mars or
something.

'Anyway, Ell, why didn't you show up at Em's party?' asks
Rachel.

'Oh, I don't know, I don't really like parties that much,' I
say. 'I never know what to wear or what to do.'

'Do? What d'you mean *do*? You don't *do* anything. You just wait for things to happen to you.'

'There's never anyone I want things to happen with, let alone *do* things with.'

'Oh yeah,' laughs Becks. 'We know. What about all the blokes in your footie team – Touchers and Feelers United? What goes on in the changing rooms?'

'Nothing! Anyway, I'm the only one in the Ladies,' I say almost crossly. 'And I don't fancy any of the team, especially as they were all crap on Saturday.'(Now, if I was strapped to a lie detector, with electrodes attached to my most sensitive parts and the power turned up to maximum, no doubt it would discover that my second-to-last comment was not completely and altogether true – but why should I tell them that?)

'Not even Adam, the-most-beautiful-boy-in-the-world's brother? I think he's quite cute.'

'Oh, he's all right,' I lie again, going slightly red. 'I haven't really got time for all that.'

They look at me all funny again – like they don't believe me – like I'm telling porkies. Just as they're about to quiz me further, Claudie Simmons-Dunne (rather stuck-up with a bad lisp) crosses over, and starts the whole blasted thing up again.

'Who thnogged who? How far did they let whoever it wath go? How much booze did they manage to pour down their *thwoaths*? Who texthted who in the morning? *Who'th* theeing who again?' All that kind of thtuff.

It's all so boring. Who cares? It's like they've got one-track minds – and everyone knows where all their tracks end up. The trouble is, if you try and change the subject, they think you're weird.

Just in time, Beth draws alongside and we split from the others.

'Hi sweet, how you doing?' I say. 'I've just had my ears bent back by the junior sex maniacs club for a few hours. It's all they ever talk about.'

'I'm so glad we didn't go to that party. Not that my parents would have let me.'

'Not sure mine would,' I say. 'Not if there were going to be any of the dreaded male species lurking about.'

'I'm sure Mum and Dad reckon I'd be a teenage mother and bride in exactly nine months.'

'You can't get married at fourteen.'

Beth throws me one of her world-famous weary looks and carries on. 'I wouldn't mind, but I couldn't bear doing anything in front of everyone else.'

'What – too public?'

'I suppose so. Luckily, you don't tend to get that many orgies in Rainsfield – let alone Tudor Close. Anyway, I reckon we had a wicked time on Saturday, without all that lot.'

'Did we?' I enquire. 'Where did we go? Was I there? I'm sure I'd remember any orgy. Oh, you mean the football club.'

'Yeah! I think it's quite cool being the only girls.'

'I bet you do. You were really hitting on my brother big time.'

Beth looks slightly embarrassed but even so, she can't let it lie.

'Ell, do you think he likes me?'

'Yeah, I think so. But it's hard to tell with him – he gets on with everyone.'

'Does he say much?'

'About what?'

'About me.'

'He said he thinks you're dead funny.'

'Funny? Is that all?'

'Well . . .'

I desperately try to think of something else.

'See,' she says gloomily, 'that's what most boys think. They all think I'm funny and stuff, but all the ones that want to take me out, aren't.'

'Aren't what?'

'Funny.'

'Billy Dawson's quite funny,' I say brightly. 'He wrote you that note – and you reckon that Valentine, last year, came from him.'

'Billy Dawson fancies anything with a pulse. Anyway, about ten girls got cards with exactly the same thing on.'

'I didn't,' I say, almost sadly. I fancy Billy Dawson as much as I fancy the Prime Minister, but that's not the point . . . I'd rather have a card from him than no one (which is exactly who I *did* get a card from).

'I reckon you're the lucky one,' says Beth sulkily. 'Anyway, you always make out you're not that interested.'

'How's the diet going?' I ask, realising this particular subject's doomed.

'It's not. I got fed up with all that rich food, and Mum found out what I was doing.'

'She won't tell your dad will she?'

'No way.'

'Did you lose any weight?'

'I did a bit, but put it all back on in spots. That's greasy food for you. That bloke that invented it must have ended up one big ball of grease. Anyway, I found out he weighed eighteen stone when he died.'

'Why don't you do some circuit training with us on Saturday? We usually do it just before a game.'

'You're joking. They'd all take the piss.'

'No way, Jose. They all really like you – honest.'

'Come on then – tell me. What exactly do you do?'

'Well, let's see, we all do sort of warm-up stuff first – bending over, touching our toes, a few press-ups and all that, and then run we round the outside of the pitch a bit till we're all loose and ready to kick the ball about.'

'I reckon I'd be ready to lie down for a week – with or without the flipping ball.'

'Don't be stupid. Look, just turn up and do what you can. Anyway, Jamie will be there.'

'OK, Ell. Stop taking the piss. Anyway, I wouldn't want *him* to see me like that. Look, I do really like him. I think about him all the time. He's different from the others.'

'Yeah, I agree. That's only because he's lucky enough to be my brother. If he wasn't, I reckon *I'd* fancy him.'

Thank God he is. The last thing I need is to have a fight with my best mate over a bloke – any bloke.

Battles With My Mum

Time to tackle Mum. She's in the kitchen. Now then, how shall I approach this one? I know . . . flattery. That always works. Well, most times.

'Hi, Mum. Mmmm! That smells delish. What we having?'

'Just pasta. Same as usual on Mondays.'

'Oh brilliant – my favourite. Especially the way you do it. How was work today? Sell many paintings?' (Mum works for this rather smart art gallery in Hampstead.)

'No, we never do much on a Monday. Even rich people seem to blow all their pocket-money over the weekend.'

'Oh, that's a shame.'

'Hang on a minute, young lady. Why the great concern? What are you after?'

Oh no! Methinks my cover's blown.

'Oh nothing, Mum. Just asking, that's all.'

'Are you sure?'

'Honest, nothing.'

'Ella Furgusson, speak now or for ever hold your peace.'

'Well . . . there was just one smallish thing?'

'Aha – here it comes.'

'It's just that . . . well, there's going to be this huge Valentine Ball at the town hall. Everyone's going.'

Mum smiles knowingly, but doesn't look up. 'That's nice, darling.'

'It's for a really good cause – to raise money to do up the

leisure centre. They're going to have a swimming pool. It's got The Fugitives and Will Bradley playing.'

'Oh, I see.'

Mum carries on stirring the sauce, as if that's the end of it. I realise I have to carry on stirring as well.

'Er . . . it's just that Beth and I wanted to go.'

Mum stops in mid-stir and gives me one of those rather sad-eyed, why-does-my-little-girl-have-to-grow-up? looks. She does this whenever I show any signs of wanting to do things that other girls of anywhere near my age do. At this rate I'll be single till I'm about ninety and Mum will still be telling me who I can and who I can't go out with from the grave.

'Don't you think you're a little young? Hannah told me about it and it sounds rather grown up for you. I wasn't too wild about her going actually. You've never been to anything like that before, Ella darling.'

Amazing! Mum's just stumbled over the whole point. This is going to be harder work than I first thought.

'So you *do* know about it?' I say. 'Anyway, that's just it, Mum. I am a proper teenager, even if you hadn't noticed.'

'What about Beth? What did her mother have to say about it?'

'Oh – er – she said it was fine,' I say rather too casually.

Mum looks slightly taken aback.

'Oh really, I'm surprised. Are you sure, Ella?'

This is showing all the usual signs of falling apart. I realise I have to push on pretty quick.

'So, can I . . . ?'

'In that case,' she interrupts, 'you won't mind me phoning and asking her about it then?'

'Who?'

'Beth's mother.'

'Er . . . well she didn't exactly use the word "fine".'

'So, pray tell, what exact word did she use?'

'Well, I'm not quite sure.'

'But she did say Beth could go.'

'Well, not exactly, but Beth's pretty sure she will.'

'Oh I see. So, in other words, she knows nothing about it.'

'Well, I wouldn't say "nothing" exactly. Oh please, Mum. I promise I won't smoke or drink or take mind-altering drugs or go off with murderers and I promise I'll be home before I get there.'

'What time? What time does this thing go on till?'

'The poster said one o'clock or something.'

'There's no way we're letting you out till one o'clock. Eleven's quite late enough.'

'Oh Muuuuum! What can happen to me between eleven and one that can't happen before?'

'My point exactly. That's why I didn't want you to go in the first place.'

'What about twelve?'

'I said eleven.'

(Brilliant! She said eleven. Yippeee!!! I think I've got her. I can't come home at eleven if I haven't even been there at all.)

'Does that mean I *can* go?'

'I never said that. You're trying to trick me. You'll have to ask your father.'

Deep Thought for the Day

I reckon the two most used phrases in the English language are 'You'll have to ask your father' and 'You'll have to ask your mother.'

'You always say that,' I continue, desperately. 'And he'll always say no, if you've said no.'

'Well, that saves me having to say it twice then, doesn't it?'

'Oh Muuum!'

'Don't "Oh Mum" me.'

'What if we went with someone older and more sensible?'

'Like who? Please don't say your sister.'

'What about Jamie?'

'He wouldn't want to go to a thing like that. Does he know anything about it?'

'Yes, and he's agreed – really this time – honest. Look, can't you ask Dad nicely? Pleeease, Mum.'

'Oh well – we'll see.'

'You always say that too.'

Mum tries a different tack completely, but I can tell she realises that she's getting the worst of this. I feel just like a tiger must feel, going in for the kill.

'Hannah says it's a bit formal,' she says. 'Long dresses and everything. You haven't got anything remotely like that.'

'I've sorted that out.'

'Are you planning to wear some of my clothes?'

I nearly say, 'Why on earth would I want to do that?' but think better of it in the circumstances.

'Then I suppose you'll be wanting to wear make-up,' Mum bleats on.

'Mum, you can't keep me in rompers all my life. It's bad enough now.'

'It's just that you've never seemed that interested in that sort of thing before.'

'That's just what I've been trying to say. I haven't, and I suppose I'm not that much now. I'm only really interested in the music. Will Bradley's my favourite in the whole world. Oh please, Mum, just say that you think it'll be OK.'

'Well, all right, but only if your father agrees.'

'And can I be home by twelve?'

'Eleven.'

'Twelve – please.'

'Eleven-thirty, that's my last offer.'

'What's in half an hour? That's ridiculous.'

Mum stops stirring again and turns and faces me. Yikes, anyone would think I was asking to go to fight in a war or join the National Front youth club or something.

'OK, Ella Furgusson, this is my very final offer – but only if your father agrees. You can go to this ball thing if 1) Beth's going, with the permission of her parents, 2) if Jamie will go with you and keep an eye on you both – ALL evening, 3) if you promise to leave dead on twelve o'clock.'

'I won't be able to leave if I'm dead.'

'Ella, stop now! Please don't push your luck. You know full well what I mean. And I want you picked up either by Dad or me or Beth's parents.'

'Thanks, Mum. Ooh! Dad's just come in. I'll go and tell

47

him that you said it's OK.'

'Hey wait a minute, I didn't say it's . . .'

Another Deep Thought for the Day

What planet do parents come from? They have this idea that the minute it gets dark and we're out of their immediate vision, we're going to turn into a crack-sniffing, sex-crazed alcoholics. They've only got to ask themselves why they didn't go over the top when they were younger (if they were younger) and they'd realise how daft it is to presume we will.

Quick call to Beth.

'Beth, guess what? I talked Mum into it. She says I can go.'

Beth's quiet for a second.

'Lucky cow. My mum's just said a flat "no". She said I'm too young and that's it.'

'Don't panic, I'm not going without you – I wouldn't dare. Mum was suddenly a lot keener when I mentioned Jamie.'

'That didn't seem to help me. Mine just went on and on about you and me being too young.'

'Do you think I should get my mum to ring yours?'

'Would she? Could she do it soonish?'

'I'll ask her to now. If she doesn't ring, say, in the next twenty-four hours, get yours to ring her.'

'OK, but I don't give out much hope. It's a right bummer.'

'Keep everything crossed.'

'I think that's what my mum'll say, especially if we ever get to go.'

We both laugh our wickedest laughs.

I love my mate Beth.

I call for Beth on the way to school the following morning. She seems all excited and can't stop jigging about. When we get outside her front gate she starts: 'I was going to ring you last night, but by the time I finished yabbering to my mum, she said it was too late and I had to go straight to bed.'

'What happened?'

'Your mum rang.'

'She did? What happened?'

'Well, it was me who answered the phone, so I knew it was her. She and Mum must have gone on for yonks. It drove me crazy, I could only hear bits and pieces.'

'And?'

'Do you want the good news or the bad news?'

'Oh hell, give me the bad news. We might as well get it over with.'

'Aha! There isn't any! Mum said YES!'

'She said YES! You're taking the p ... WOW! That's *sooooooo* wicked. My good old mum! I knew she'd turn out all right in the end.'

'I think I might have to sign a thirty-page list of conditions in my virgin blood, though.'

'Like what?'

'Oh you know – no drinking, no looking happy, no heavy breathing, that sort of stuff. Oh yeah and no making-out in the loos.'

'Yeah, same with me. I think I might have to be handcuffed to Jamie.'

'Wish I could be. That's the only way I'll ever get close to him, I reckon. But, hey, who cares? We're almost going to the ball, ha ha. We've just got to get el dosho together. Did you ask your mum about the sale?'

'Not yet, I thought I'd let her get over this lot first. Mind you, compared to the first battle, I think it'll be dead easy.'

'What are we going to wear? I haven't got anything vaguely smart.'

'I still wish I could go in jeans.'

'You can't – you'd look stupid, anyway that poster said you had to dress up.'

'What for? I look better in those sort of clothes.'

'How do you know if you've never tried? I'm going to do the works – high-heels, make-up and everything. If you want to look like a bloke you can, but don't stand next to me.'

'Oh all right – keep your knickers untwisted. Trouble is, I don't know where to start. I've never even tried before. There's no way I'm going to ask Hannah.'

Beth suddenly looks worried.

'How long have I got to make myself slim, sophisticated and utterly ravishing?'

'Not long enough. About the same time as I've got to learn how to pull guys . . . and grow my hair.'

'That bit's easy.'

'I reckon I'll start pulling hard every night.'

'What – guys?'

'No. Hair, silly.'

Beth starts bouncing up and down on the spot in a rather curious manner.

'And it's circuit training on Friday, isn't it?'

'Careful, Beth, we mustn't take it too far, we have to give the others a chance – it's only fair, darling.'

'What's fair got to do with it? If I've got to bounce my boobs off and live on flipping lettuce leaves and squeezed carrots, I don't care what the others do.'

'Seriously, Beth, how are we going to do all the rest of it – hair and make-up and stuff? I've only worn a bit of lippy once, and that was in the school play.'

Beth suddenly stands stock-still and looks as if she's wet herself.

'Ell, I nearly forgot! I must be going loopy. That's the other thing I had to tell you. Take a deep breath. I'm afraid there's more good news.'

'*More?* I don't know if I can get my head round more.'

'You know I told you that my mum used to be a hair and make-up artist before she married my dad?'

'Yeah, sort of.'

'She used to do ads and stuff for cosmetic companies and magazines. She was on a shoot over in South Africa, when she met him in a hospital lobby. She'd injured her foot and had been taken to casualty. My dad was on duty . . .'

'Too-much-information alert. Get on with it.'

'So, she said that if we were going to go to this thing, she'd rather I did it properly. She said she didn't want us going out looking like a couple of kids who didn't know what we were doing. Professional pride, I think it's called.'

51

'You are so not serious?'

'I so am. And get this, *mon amie*. Then she suddenly got properly serious. I thought for one minute she was going to give me bloody lecture on under-age sex.'

'Did she?'

'No, she said that not only will she do our hair and make-up for the ball but something much better. She said, in a dead straight voice, that "the time has come".'

'Jeez! For what?'

'To teach me – that means us – how to do make-up ourselves, properly. Not just ordinary, like everyone else does, but all the tricks of the trade . . . and . . .!'

'There's more?'

'Much! She said that there are a couple of big cases up in the loft, full up with more make-up than we'll ever need in our lifetimes. It was from when she was a professional, so it's good gear – oh yeah, and all the brushes and tweezers and stuff she used to use. The big make-up companies used to send her all their new products as freebies to try. She said we can share them all out.'

'Will it still be OK?'

'Yeah, she said most of it's never been opened. There's bound to be loads of everything, she said.'

'When can we have it?'

'After she's done our make-up and taught us how to do it ourselves.'

'We must get someone to take our photos.'

'I'll ring the big fashion magazines – they'll fight over the chance.'

'Oh yeah – more like *Farmers' Weekly*.'

Beth suddenly looks cross.

'Are you talking about me again?'

'Beth! Will you shut it! J for joke, or what? You wait, with a bit of fine-tuning you'll look amazing. Sorry sweet, you *do* look amazing, but with the full works you'll look even amazinger. Anyway, what about me? I've just got to avoid looking like a stick with a painted knob on top.'

Another Deep Thought for the Day

You never know when you're going to be interested in things. I mean, I've never really thought of wearing make-up and looking pretty before, but suddenly it seems more important than almost anything else (except footie).

'I c-can't believe you d-do this for pleasure, Ell.'

It's Friday evening and Beth's just finished her very first bout of circuit training. She's bright red and puffing like a . . . like a puffing thing.

'It'll get better the more you do it – honest. Isn't that right, Jamie?'

'You bet. Anyway, Beth, I thought you did really well. Really.'

'You have to be joking. How come I look like a tomato and sound like a hot collie?'

'I like tomatoes . . . and collies,' he comes back. 'Anyway, it's good to get up a sweat. It means it was aerobic or whatever they call it.'

'It's all right for you, Jamie. You look like you've just

walked downstairs and you've done more than me.'

'I bet if you keep this up and do a bit every night, Beth, you'll be really fit in a few weeks.'

Poor old Beth looks slightly gloomy again.

'If not, you can bury my exhausted and emaciated body in a little narrow grave where I fall over.'

'No pain, no gain,' I say rather smugly.

'No cash, no bash you mean,' says Beth. 'Have you asked your mum and dad yet about the garage sale?'

'Yeah, last night. I thought they might be annoyed, but actually they didn't seem to mind the idea, as long we make it plain that we're doing it for us, not them. It was really funny. Mum said it was a chance for Dad to get rid of all the junk in the garage, and Dad said it was a chance to get rid of all the clothes she never wears. By the time they'd finished, I could see Dad living in the garage and Mum prowling around totally starkers.'

'So can we start getting stuff together?' asks Jamie.

'Sure thing. We can start with Gran's on Saturday. I rang her and she said she's going to sort out a load for us. Then she said we can delve around in her attic. She's got no idea what we'll find up there.'

Jamie starts to giggle.

'I hope we won't find her brother – grumpy Eric. Do you remember Dad telling us about our great-uncle Eric? He's the one who disappeared without trace. Gran said he went out to get a paper twenty years ago and never came back.'

'What if she really did bump him off?'

I break in with an even gigglier giggle.

'Look, don't knock it, Jamie, we could get quite a lot for a good skeleton. I read once they go for hundreds.'

'I reckon that's what I'll be after all this lot,' moans Beth, still gasping from her exertions.

I really wish I could ask Adam to help us – but we still haven't spoken since our row.

Dad says we can store all the things we collect in the bit of the garage that isn't filled with the stuff he point-blank refuses to get rid of. I start the ball rolling with Hannah's Cindy dolls, which she hasn't looked at for years, and the little pink bike with stabilisers that I had for my fourth birthday. Jamie's Action Men look like they've been through a sort of plastic holocaust (and lost). Some have arms missing, some legs, and one poor bloke is just a headless, armless torso with his gun attached to him by an elastic band. It reminds me of some of the stuff we saw at the Imperial War Museum when we went with the school.

Beth brings a warrior's shield (without warrior, thank God) that her dad brought back from Africa one time, a signed photo of Jerry Hall – who was one of the first super-models. There's also one of those imitation lifelike cats made with real fur that you can kick across the room and upset your rellies with, and a machine that wakes you up with a cup of tea in the morning (I prefer butlers, personally).

My mum and dad's collection is weirder. You can almost trace their whole married life through it. Dad's given us one of those foldaway workbenches that Mum had bought him one Christmas when they'd just got married, hoping he'd do things round the house. He turned out to be the worst DIY man in history and in the end only used the vice bit for getting the tops off beer bottles. Then there's one of those trouser-press thingies and best of all, a fish on a plaque that turns to face you and sings *Take Me to the River*. Someone bought it as a joke for poor old Dad when he didn't manage to catch anything on his first (and last) fly-fishing trip (I used to think they were going off to catch flies, when I was little).

Jamie's done some brilliant posters on his computer and copied them on the school copier. We're going to put them up all round the nearby streets. Mum's suggested that we can give free tea and coffee to the customers. It's so fab, I can't see how we can fail.

My Old Gran

It's only a couple of weeks to go before 'The Sale of the Century'. Beth rang the local paper and told them we were having a sale in aid of the leisure centre appeal (they wouldn't have been interested if we'd only mentioned that we wanted the money for tickets). One of the reporters actually came round (a rather posh girl with a bad haircut) and interviewed us about it. *Teenage Initiative* or some crap like that, they're going to call it. That's if they run it at all.

Jamie and I have whizzed round to our gran's to see what she's going to let us flog. She still lives in the same big house in Chestnut Avenue (just round the corner) that my dad was brought up in . . . but now, as she has trouble getting up the stairs, she's decided to get one of those flats where someone can keep an eye on you. My brother and I were a bit pissed off at first because we wanted her to get one of those stair-lift thingies, so we could have a go. Could that possibly be regarded as selfish?

Anyway, she greets us with big kisses.

'If there's anything you can see that you think you can sell, put it to one side. My new place has only got two rooms and a kitchen, so I can hardly take anything. You'd be doing me a favour. I'm moving in three weeks.'

'What about Skippy?' Jamie asks, looking down at the straggly yellow thing at his ankles. Skippy's her ancient and deeply smelly West Highland White terrier.

'They don't usually allow pets, but they said, as he's so very old, they'd make an exception. Otherwise I'd have to have him put down. I told them they should put me down too and save everybody the trouble and expense.'

Jamie gives her a really sweet hug.

'Gran, don't be daft. Dead grans are no use to us.'

'And we wouldn't even be able to sell you at our sale – or Skippy,' I add, knowing she won't take it the wrong way.

Gran giggles and then gives me a big hug in case I feel left out. She really is the coolest old person in the universe. It's as if her insides have stayed all right while all the bits that you see have worn out (a bit like a threadbare old teddy bear, Jamie once said). Anyway, I tell her all about the Valentine's Ball and why we have to get the money.

'You're as daft as brushes, you two. Why didn't you come to me? I'd have given it to you. What else have I got to spend money on these days, apart from my sky-diving lessons?'

'Sky-diving?' we both yell in chorus.

'Only joking,' she says, laughing. 'I was reading about it this morning in the paper. How much do you need?'

'Seriously, Gran,' says Jamie, 'thanks tons, but Ell and I want to do this on our own. That's what the sale's all about.'

'OK, darling, if you insist. Now let me see . . . most of what's in this room I'll probably be able to take, but more or less everything else I'll be glad to see the back of. All they do is harbour dust and distant memories. I want to look forward to my new little home without being dragged back to the past every five minutes. That's the trouble with being ancient.

Tell you what – why don't you stack everything you want in one of the spare bedrooms, until your dad can come round in the car and pick it all up.'

Deep Thought for the Day

I suddenly got to thinking how sad it is that our bodies get worn out. Our gran's quicker than most of us when it comes to getting the point of something. But now she's in her late seventies she's getting pretty doddery and I don't think that's fair. I once asked Gran if she minded being old and she said something really clever. She said people only really worry about age when they see the first signs of it. When you actually are old, she said, it doesn't really matter any more. How wise is that?

Jamie and I are up in Gran's attic sifting through lots of old boxes and tea chests. Luckily there's a little window in the roof, so we can see quite clearly.

'Hey, Ell, come and look at this. It's an old photo album. It's full of pictures of Mum and Dad. Look, here's one of Dad as a teenager. He must be about my age.'

'Jeez, what a wally. I knew he went to a smart school, but I didn't know it was that smart. What a stupid outfit.'

'And look at the hair. How naff is that!'

'Hey, here's one of Dad with a girl. She looks quite cool . . . for him! I wonder what happened to her? Hang on a mo. It's not Mum, is it?'

'Where? Who her? Never! Mum was never blonde – or a babe . . . was she? What does it say at the bottom?'

I squint in the dusty light.

'"Roy and Christina – Cambridge." Blimey, Ell, it *is* her.'

'Mum looks so much older than Dad.'

'She is, by a couple of years.'

'I always wondered why she calls him her "Roy Boy". Geddit? That's her idea of a joke.'

'No wonder Gran keeps this book in the attic,' I say.

'Turn over the page.'

I whip over the page rather excitedly. Jamie looks puzzled.

'You can tell this one's a bit later – Dad looks the same, but Mum looks like she's swallowed a horse.'

I look closer.

'Jamie! Don't be daft, she's pregnant. What does it say?'

'"Christina and Roy – expecting a happy event."'

'It's bloody you in there,' yells Jamie, almost falling over backwards with exaggerated laughter.

'How do you work that out?' I say. 'How come it's in the back garden of the old house. I was born in the house we're in now.'

Jamie studies the photo with even more of a look of horror on his face, like he's looking at an alien or something. I wonder about him sometimes. I don't know how he reckons he came into the world – brought by a stork or found under a gooseberry bush knowing him.

'That's so gross. Mum walking about like that with me inside her.'

'Like what?'

'Like all fat and stuff.'

'Jamie!' I yell. 'What do you expect, you knob-head? You didn't think she carried you in a rucksack, did you? Maybe you think she ought to have been kept in a locked room till you were ready for your grand entrance?'

Jamie suddenly points to a photo that's loose in one of the folders.

'Hey, Ell, look at this one. Who the hell's that? Now she really is a babe.'

'It's much older than the others. It's in black and white.'

I look at it closely, but it has nothing written underneath. The picture shows a beautiful girl of about eighteen or so with a long neck and short dark hair, cut in a sort of bob. She's got really heavy eyeshadow and what looks like bright red lips (as far as you can tell in black and white).

'She looks a bit like you, Ell . . . a bit.'

'You what? Blimey, time for an eye test, Jamie. Who is it? Let's ask Gran when we go back down.'

We eventually go downstairs to find Gran picking some roses in the back garden.

'Gran, we found this picture up in the attic. Who is it?'

Gran narrows her old eyes and squints at the photo. She looks up slowly with a strange faraway expression on her face and a faint, proud smile.

'You'd never guess, my dears, when you look at this poor broken-down old thing now, but that was me on my seventeenth birthday.'

We both look from her to the photo and back again, mouths open, and realise that beneath the spider's web of tiny wrinkles, and the white hair and glasses, there are traces of the girl in the picture.

'You look amazing, Gran,' I say, almost in a whisper. 'What was the photo taken for?'

'I was going to my first dance. Like your ball, in a way. It was the first time I ever wore make-up.'

'What was your dress like?' I ask. 'I can't really see clearly from the photo.'

'It was long and sleek in black silk, with tiny matching seed pearls sewn on to the bodice. It was high at the front and buttoned up the back. It was the most beautiful dress I've ever seen before or since.'

'It must have cost tons,' murmurs Jamie, ever practical.

'Well, it would have done, but my father – that would be your great-grandad – worked for a very swanky department store in the West End and they said I could borrow it, if I would model some gowns for the dress department's fashion show.'

I look at my granny and realise that though she's stooped and little now, she must have been quite tall when she was younger.

'And did you do it?' I ask.

'Not only that,' she says, proudly, 'but I went on to model for a top Bond Street fashion house for a few years. That was before I met your grandfather.'

'You were a model?' I say in awe. 'Mum and Dad never told us that.'

'I might not even have told them, dear.'

'What was it like?' I ask.

'Oh, it was nothing like it is now, running around with practically nothing on, showing everything you've got. In those days, it was a very respectable career.'

'Isn't it now?' asks Jamie.

'Not the way you hear about these – what do you call them? Supermodels – carrying on.'

'Gran, may I keep this photo?' I ask.

'As long as you don't sell it at your sale, darling.'

Horrid Hannah

It doesn't take long for Hannah to get wind of Beth and my plans to go to the ball. She corners me after school one day.

'Mum's just told me that the rumour I heard is right. You and Beth really are going to that thing at the town hall.'

'If we can get the money together – sure – why not?'

'Well, I suppose I can't do much about it. Do what you want, but don't go showing me up.'

'Like how?'

'Like coming up and asking me things and all that.'

'Like all what? What would I want to ask you?'

'Oh, I don't know. You might just start hanging around, that sort of thing.'

'OK. So what you're actually saying, yeah, is that you won't want to know me.'

'Look, Ella, it's just that it's an important night for me. I'm being taken by Greg Cresswell.'

'Greg Cresswell! How did you wangle that?'

'Oh, he just kept on at me. You know how it is.'

She twiddles her hair and looks down to the ground with one of those soppy coy faces, like butter wouldn't melt in her mouth.

'Well, don't worry about me and Beth,' I break in. 'The last thing we'll want to do is get in the way. We might get hurt.'

I tell Beth about it the following day and she seems surprised as well. Greg Cresswell could have anyone he wanted.

Perhaps he sees something in Hannah we don't.

As for Adam, I've been avoiding him at footie, because I don't know quite what to say, and now I've just heard that Jamie's invited him to the ball with us. What does all this mean?

Now, as far as the sale's concerned, the garage is beginning to fill up nicely. Mrs Heath, the old lady from next door, says she made far too much jam last year and told us we could sell it. I'll say she made too much, you could practically spread the whole of Rainsfield with it. I say to Beth that it's beginning to sound more like a church fete than a boot sale.

'We could have a coconut shy like they have at fairs,' she giggles.

'And a beer tent.'

'And a merry-go-round for the kids.'

'What about Dodgem cars?' I suggest.

'And a big wheel.'

'Yeah, and we could invite the Red Arrows.'

'And get the Queen to open it.'

By this time we're rolling about on the sofa.

'Or the Prime Minister, even,' I say, determined not to lose the thread. 'We must tell the TV stations.'

'From all over the world,' adds Beth.

'Tell you what,' I say, 'I've got a better idea. Let's make it really exclusive and keep it to ourselves. Let's not even tell the press.'

'Too late,' says Beth, 'that thing's in the paper tomorrow, so that reporter said.'

'OK, we'll just ban film stars and famous people.'

'Yeah, right. Good job we haven't posted a letter to the Queen. It would have been dead tricky getting out of it.'

'Yeah – all those carriages jammed up in our street.'

'Think of all the poo.'

'Poo?' I say. 'What are you on about?'

'From the horses, silly.'

'What about the Prime Minister – he'll do his nut when he hears he can't come. 'We must get our people to send his people some money to make up for it.' I suggest. 'Fifty grand should just about do it.'

'What about his wife?'

'OK, a hundred, but that's my final offer.'

And so it goes – on and on and on . . . that's the trouble with us, once we've started we can't seem to stop.

Beth sleeps over so that she, Jamie and I can get an early start in the morning. We have to put the piles of stuff, now practically filling the garage, on the trestle tables that Dad had to hire. Last night we put little price stickers on everything. I even stuck one on our cat Roger in case anyone might be silly enough to buy her, but Mum took it off and cuddled the poor thing, as if I was really planning to go through with it. You might well be wondering why our lady cat's called Roger. We didn't know she was a girl, see, when we got her, and only found out when she got pregnant by next door's cat called Blackie (cos he's black!). We decided that she'd probably got used to the name Roger so it stuck.

Mum and Dad help with the pricing, but Dad insists on

whipping away a few things which he reckons might be quite valuable. The signed picture of Jerry Hall could be very sought after, he says, and also he's heard of people who'll pay good money for African Crafts. Most valuable of all, he thinks, is an ancient and slightly scruffy tin train set, German he reckons, that belonged to his dad. It's still in the original box which means it's more valuable apparently. Jamie and I had found it under some old rugs in Gran's attic. Dad says he's got this old schoolmate in Fulham with an antique shop, and he's asked him to pop over and have a look at them all.

As we're laying it all out, we notice something very strange. From out of nowhere, people begin to appear.

'Where have that lot come from?' I ask.

'From the Planet Bargain, I suppose,' says Jamie.

Deep Thought for the Day

Have you ever wondered why there are so many more old ladies than old men? Dad reckons it's because men 'pop off' earlier to get away from being nagged. Mum says it's because women are the superior half of the species.

'We're supposed to open at ten-thirty, aren't we?' asks Beth, as a queue begins to form.

Ten minutes later Mum walks out with a tray of tea and toast for us workers, looking like she's not quite woken up, but soon does an about-turn when some of the people, thinking it's for them, break through and head for her like a pack of hyenas.

'Do you remember that old film *The Birds*?' says Jamie.

'It was on telly the other night. It's the one where all the birds in the world suddenly turn nasty and start hanging around outside houses waiting to get their beaks into the people indoors. They remind me of them.'

By a quarter to ten, we can't hold on much longer and we declare the sale open. Even Mum, and later Dad come out to help cope with the rush. Hannah, of course, is still in bed. Lazy cow!

'How much will you take for this?' yells one old lady, brandishing a hideous wooden table lamp from my gran's attic.

'What's your bottom price on these?' cries another, with a large box full of odd teacups marked 'fifty pence'.

'Does this still work?' asks a strange old man wearing a beret and crumpled raincoat, holding an electric iron that looks like it might have been the first ever made.

'Looks like he could do with one,' whispers Beth, who's having a tug of war with some snotty little kid who she's caught trying to nick one of Jamie's old Action Men.

A rather smart-looking bloke wearing a blazer drives up in a black Range Rover with dark windows and turns out to be Dad's old school friend. He goes into the garage with dad and after a bit comes out with an armful of stuff. We're all too busy to think any more about it.

By eleven o'clock we're totally knackered. There must have been over a hundred people, I reckon. All that's left are a few sad old Seventies records that my parents donated; some yellowing paperbacks by people nobody's ever heard of; and a pile of old faded woollies which had been about to go to Oxfam. Dad's raging on about some dodgy-looking man who'd found some of his tools by the back door and was asking how much he wanted for them.

After the last of the customers have disappeared with their purchases, we begin to add up what we've taken.

'I've got £57.35,' utters Jamie in a shocked voice.

'I've got £48.50,' says my mum.

I have to count mine again.

'Sixty-one ninety-five,' I murmur, hardly believing what I'm saying.

'I just managed £35.87,' says Dad defensively, 'but I was only out for half an hour or so.'

Beth looks completely awestruck.

'You're never going to believe this, but I've just counted £87.03.'

'Why don't you keep the three pence for yourself,' says Jamie.

Dad fetches his calculator and tots it up.

'Well, kiddy-winks, I think you just might be able to go to the ball. You've made nearly three hundred pounds.'

He then holds his hand up to silence us.

'Hang on a sec, I think you're all forgetting my friend, Charles. He said that some of the stuff in the garage was really quite valuable. He and his partner run a general auction in Chelsea on Tuesdays. He said he'd put them in and not take any commission, as it's for charity.'

Beth, Jamie and I look at each other with open mouths.

Dad continues, 'I think you three should take whatever you need for your tickets, plus the cost of hiring clothes, and a bit for all your expenses and then the rest can go to the leisure centre appeal.'

For one moment I feel ever so slightly cheated. Why can't Beth, Jamie and me have *all* the money – it was our idea, after all? Then I realise that people like my gran and Beth's dad had donated their stuff without a thought of reward, and that some bloke who we've never met is selling those things with no profit for himself. I'm so glad I managed to keep my big mouth shut.

As it turns out, some of the stuff was worth quite a bit. The signed photo of Jerry Hall was bought by a friend of my dad's for seventy-five pounds, while some nutter paid two hundred and fifty pounds for the train set. The thing that shocked everyone, however, was that old battered tribal shield. An expert said it was definitely Zulu and so old and rare that it could be worth a lot. Dad rang Beth's dad and asked him if he wanted it back (like, yeah!) but he said that it should go to auction and that he would donate the proceeds to the Rainsfield Leisure Centre appeal. A few days later it was bought by some museum for two and a half grand! That's Zulus for you.

Free Tickets and High-heeled Shoes

It's a week or so later. Dad's just had a letter from this bloke on the committee of the leisure centre appeal – the chairman, I think he said. It's about all that money we sent them. I ring Beth as soon as he's shown it to me.

'Beth, guess what? Something stupendously ridiculoso has just happened.'

'Don't tell me, you and Adam got married.'

'Don't be a dork. He doesn't even think I like him any more. In fact, I think he thinks the opposite. No, it's even better than that, if you can believe such a thing. Hang on while I read you this letter that came to my dad. Are you ready?'

'How come you're reading your dad's letters?'

'Shut up and listen. You'll see. The letter's from this man called Derek Norrington, chairman of the Rainsfield Leisure Centre appeal.

Dear Mr Furgusson,

The committee and I were delighted by your generous donation to our appeal. You mentioned in your letter that this was mostly the work of your two teenage children and the daughter of Mr Henry Middleton, whose own donation was most spectacular. The sale you held to raise the money was originally, you say, simply to buy tickets to our

forthcoming charity ball. Please accept, on our behalf, and with
enormous gratitude, three special tickets to our ball, admitting
the holders to the VIP lounge which we are setting up for
important guests and local personalities. This will include the
performers who will be playing that evening. We feel it is the least
we can do. All refreshments will, of course, be at our expense.

Thank you once again and let me assure you that you will
be hearing from us when we celebrate the re-opening of our
much improved and long-awaited leisure centre.'

The line goes dead for a few seconds, then Beth speaks in a
slightly wobbly voice.

'Hold on. Does that mean – ? Have I heard you right?'

'It means we should even get to meet Will Bradley! And
Dad said we can hang on to the ticket money.'

'Jeez, Ell, how wicked's that? What are we going to spend
it on?'

'Search me. I really, really don't know. Come round at
once. This needs a summit conference.'

Fifteen minutes later Beth turns up, out of breath.

'Hey Beth, what took you so long? I've only just put the
phone down. I bet you couldn't have done that a few weeks
ago.'

'I've never had this much money before, to spend just on
me. I nearly spent it a hundred times over in my head on the
way here. Each time I think of something I really want, I
think of something else I really want more.'

'Me too. I'll probably end up buying nothing, just because
I can't make up my stupid mind.'

'At least we don't have to buy make-up,' she says. 'What about shoes? I haven't got anything remotely sexy.'

'You could borrow my other footie boots.'

'Very funny. I tried walking in some of my mum's old stilettos the other day, from when she was younger. They were a bit big, but you could get the general idea. It was like walking on stilts.'

'I reckon we should get some shoes pretty soon, so we can practise. We can't stroll into high society and fall flat on our new, extremely beautiful faces.'

'Oh, I don't know. At least it'd get us noticed.'

'Shall we nip into town after school tomorrow?' I suggest.

'Won't those sort of shoes look a bit daft with our uniforms?'

'Yeah, you're not wrong, but we haven't got time to mess about, the ball's only a couple weeks away. We can call in at Posh Frocks as well.'

'Have you thought about what sort of dress you want?'

'Not really. The only thing I thought was that I couldn't think of any – so I thought I would choose black.'

'Maybe we'll get a better idea when we see what they've got.'

Deep Thought for the Day

I once heard someone say that there are few problems that money can't make better. I have to admit that having cash in my pocket is fab. The trouble is, I also remember being told by my grandad that a fool and his money are soon parted. Sorry, Grandad, but this particular fool can't wait.

The trip into town was quite good. Beth was right, we looked totally soppy tottering (and giggling) around shoe shops in our school uniform and high-heeled shoes. Although we'd decided that we couldn't really buy anything until we had found our dresses, one of the shops, Mortons, had some really sexy, medium-high strappy shoes which we both liked and which didn't cost a bomb. They came in black, red or silver and had those thin heels – like you see in the fashion magazines at the dentist's – all sort of flat-like.

'I still think I'd quite like a black dress of some description,' I said as we were heading for Posh Frocks.

'Suits me,' replied Beth. 'My mum always told me I'd look good in a red dress, cos of my black hair and dark colouring. I'll have the red shoes to match. Anyway, silver's a bit common. It's what lap-dancers wear.'

When we get there, Beth hits the jackpot almost instantly. She finds this wicked flame-red party dress, with a huge swirly skirt nearly to the ground and a neckline that makes my eyes water. Body-wise, she's done really well recently. She's been to our football practise every week and more than that, she's sweated it out at the school gym just about every lunch-time. I always thought she looked great, but now she looks even better – fitter somehow. The red dress pulls her in and pushes her out in all the right places.

'That looks amazing, Beth,' I say in an awestruck voice.

'I'll have to have a wrap or silk scarf or something to cover the front. It looks as if my boobs are about to fall out.'

The two women in the shop come over and repeat what I'd just said.

'You don't think I look a bit tarty, do you?' asks Beth.

'Not at all,' says the taller one, 'you've got just the sort of face to get away with it. You should try wearing your hair up.'

Her friend rushes into the back and fetches some hairpins. I don't think Beth's ever had her long black wavy hair up before – just in a pony-tail at circuit training – but when the two women have finished, she looks amazing and about a mile taller.

My hunt wasn't so successful. Everyone agreed that I should wear something long and slinky, but there was nothing that fitted me remotely. It was so disappointing. Suddenly I had this idea. I remembered how fab my gran had looked in that black silk dress in the photo, and how she'd said she'd had a figure like mine when she was young. I dashed out to the street to ring her. I told her where I was and what I was trying to do.

'Gran, I just wanted to ask you. Do you still have the dress you wore in that photo – the one we found in the attic?'

'Do you know, I was thinking about that, Ella. You must be psychic, darling. It's been in a box, wrapped in tissue paper and mothballs for over fifty years. My father's company never asked for it back, you see. Wasn't that naughty of us? I've never been able to throw it away or even sell it – it's too precious. Why, do you . . .?'

'Do you think I could try it on, Gran? We reckoned you must have been about the same size as me, right? That's if you don't mind me wearing it?'

'Of course I don't. I only ever wore it a couple of times. After your father was born, I never managed to get into it

75

again. I'd love you to wear it, darling. But won't it be rather old-fashioned?'

'You once told me that beautiful things never go out of date.'

'That's true. So when would you like to see it?'

'As soon as possible.'

'Just give me half an hour to find it, darling.'

'We'll make our way over now. It'll take that long.'

'That's fine. You can have a cup of tea and a slice of chocolate cake. I've just made it. See you soon.'

'How could anyone think of chocolate cake at a time like this?' I say to Beth, who's just joined me and is obviously wondering who the hell I'm talking to.

'How can anyone not?' she groans. 'I've been cutting right down on all that stuff and now I dream of it every night – with oodles of ice cream, and maybe a thick dollop of double . . .'

'All right, calm down and stop drooling,' I say, 'this is serious. That was Gran on the phone. She said I can wear that dress she was wearing in the picture I told you about. It's been kept in mothballs.'

'Poor moths,' says Beth, 'I never knew they had any.'

After we'd finished laughing, we hurry round to Gran's. The dress is already out of the box and draped over her sofa. It pongs of mothballs, but Gran says that if it's dry-cleaned the smell will disappear.

'You won't believe this, Ella darling, but I've checked it over and it's as good as the day I wore it. I remember having it dry-cleaned just before it went into the wardrobe.'

I stare at the dress and catch my breath, half because of the mothballs, and half because it's one of the most beautiful things I've ever seen in my short life. I pick it up almost like I would a newborn baby, in case I damage it. It's as light as a feather and I realise I've hardly ever touched pure silk, let alone thought about wearing it. I then hold it against my body. With my new heels on, it would be the perfect length – just above the floor.

'It's amazing, Gran,' I say in a voice that even I can hardly hear. 'May I try it on?'

'What do you think of this, Ella? I'm thinking of wearing it to the ball at the weekend. I borrowed it off a friend. She's going to be a model.'

It's Hannah and it's Monday evening and she's just come into my room wearing the sort of thing you see in the all those ghastly showbiz magazines – all pink and see-through and designed to show just about every part of your body (except your brains). The shoes she's wearing look suspiciously like the silver version of the ones Beth and I chose.

A model what? I *almost* say.

'Er, very nice,' I *do* say – telling a complete porkie.

'D'you think it suits me?'

'Very much,' I say – this time telling the complete truth.

'You're still thinking of going on Saturday, I suppose?' She says sneeringly. 'Mum told me about your jumble sale thingy. What are you going to wear? You do know you've got to dress up, don't you? They won't let you go in your football kit.'

'Gran lent me one of her old dresses. It's really cool.'

Hannah looks at me in disgust, like I've just let out an almighty fart.

77

'Are you joking? You *are* joking, aren't you? Please tell me you are. Look, I told you I didn't want you making me look stupid. You can't go dressed as a granny. I won't allow it.'

'I don't know how you can stop me. Look, don't worry, I told you the other day, I won't even speak to you if you don't want.' (Especially in what you're wearing, I nearly add.)

'You wait till I tell Mum you're going in fancy dress.'

'Fancy dress? I'll show you just how flipping fancy it is!'

Hannah leaves the room and I feel like I want to cry my eyes out. Why can't she ever take me seriously, or even try to help me? All my life she's treated me like a baby. Why can't she be on my side – just once, for God's sake? I can hardly believe I really wanted to be like her when I was younger. I used to copy her hair and try on her clothes when she wasn't there, but ever since she started being really nasty to me, it's all changed. I hardly talk to her if I don't have to. It's not fair – some of my friends have got big sisters who are really nice to them. Thank God I've got Jamie, that's all I can say.

If all that's not bad enough, there's the Adam situation. I don't know how to convince him I'm not a stroppy monster. And all because I didn't see that a player was offside. I'm such a creep. He was only trying to be nice and I jumped down his throat. It's really stupid, the more I think about him, the more I like him, even though I've hardly ever spoken to him properly. Maybe I'll get a chance to make things up at the ball.

Just as I feel my bottom lip beginning to wobble and my eyes fill up, the old mobe rings. Saved by the Beth, I bet!

'Hi, Ell, I just wanted to ask what your teeth look like now you've had your ironwork out?'

My braces came out this morning. After a whole year, I have a metal-free gob! I stare at the mirror to confirm that my teeth haven't gone back to how they were before.

'I'm so glad you phoned. I was about to get into a state. I've just had bloody Hannah giving me a hard time about Gran's dress.'

'What the hell's it got to do with her? She hasn't even seen you in it, has she?'

'No way! When I told her it was Gran's, she said I'd look like an old lady.'

'Since when have old ladies been wearing black, figure-hugging dresses that button up the back.'

'I didn't get a chance to mention that bit.'

'I thought it was gorge. I reckon there's only about two people in the world who could wear it and the other one was your gran – honest. Don't worry, babe, if it's not exactly right, my auntie, the one who lives round the corner, is pretty good with the old needle. She makes all her own clothes. She'd be able to make it fit in no time. I'm sure your gran will say it's OK. Anyway, why do you listen to an old boot like Hannah?'

'You should have seen what she's going to wear,' I say, beginning to cheer up. 'We wouldn't be seen dead in it.'

'Why, what's it like?'

'You know the sort of stuff those girls in the soaps wear to award ceremonies, just to get their pictures in the paper?'

'What, with all their bits hanging out?'

'Yeah! Well, it's worse than that.'

Deep Thought for the Day

What is fashion all about? If you look at the pictures from the fashion shows, they always wear things that no one in the world could get away with. You'd look mad if you wore that stuff in Rainsfield. Then again, the papers tell you that people like footballers' wives are fashionable. If that's fashion, then I'm Father Christmas.

'I tell you what,' says Beth. 'After you've asked your gran, why don't you get my Auntie Pam to take a look at it? If there's anything to be taken in or let out, she can do it by Saturday.'

'Would she really? Your family's so clever.'

'I don't quite know why,' says Beth, 'but she and my mum really want us to look amazing. I think it's because I've worked so hard at losing weight. She says she wishes she had the will-power to do it herself. Anyway, they're both getting quite excited. Auntie Pam even altered that dress from Posh Frocks a tiny bit – not that anyone would notice.'

Before and After

It's here! It's blinking ball day and suddenly I'm as nervous as a murderer going to her first execution. I've only tried the dress on once more since Gran's and that was before Beth's auntie promised to alter it. I wanted to show Mum. She went all funny and I thought for a moment she was going to cry. But what if it doesn't fit when Auntie Pam's done the alterations? Talk about last minute. What the hell will I do then? And what if Beth's mum has forgotten all she ever knew about make-up?

I search for spots on my face in Dad's shaving mirror (it's the sort that magnifies), but apart from a weeny one just under my chin, which squeezes magnificently, I'm pretty much spotless. Thank God it's not one of my world-famous ugly days. They're the ones when I wake up looking like Gollum's not-very-well daughter. Luckily, that's only usually once a month, and it isn't like that today. My hair's quite a bit longer since I decided to grow it and Beth's mum says that she thinks she can do something with it. It's ten-thirty in the morning and I can't hold on any longer. I've got to ring my best mate.

'Hi, babe, how you doing? Did you get any sleep? I hardly did.'

'Funny enough, it was OK. Last night Mum said she'd cook my favourite dinner as a treat for having done so well with my exercise, so I really pigged out big time on steak and

81

kidney pie and baked beans. I'm surprised I'm not right back to where I was – like snakes and ladders – or pigs and ladders in my case. Anyway, I always sleep well if I've eaten tons, but I feel pretty weird now. I can't believe today's finally here.'

'Me neither. And I can't believe we've gone to all this trouble. I hope your mum's as good as you say she is. We'll be right in it, otherwise. Talk about "The Ugly Sisters Go To The Ball" – I can just see the headlines.'

'Mum says she can begin teaching us properly when she makes us up this afternoon. We can all work out what suits us together. She says she's really looking forward to it. I suppose it'll be like the old days for her.'

'What time shall I come round?'

'Oh hell, Ell, as soon as you can – why hang about? It's not every day you get to be transformed into a teenage sex-goddess.'

'You wish. I reckon I'll be more like an overdressed beanpole. I haven't really told my mum we're doing this – well, not properly. I told her your mum was going to teach us make-up at some time – but not when and what for. She hasn't even seen the shoes – only the dress. If she had her way I'd still be in pink woolly booties. I think I might be getting the hang of walking in heels at last, I've been practising before I go to bed. I think I must look a bit like a page-three girl prancing around starkers with sexy shoes on. Trouble is, I feel about five metres high. There'd better be some basketball players there, otherwise I'll be like the giraffe at the very small animals' party. By the way, has your dad got a camera? Mum and Dad might not believe it unless they see it.'

'Yeah. Actually he's not bad at taking pictures. He once told me he wanted to be a photographer before he wanted to be a doctor, though I don't think it was fashion photography.'

I get all my gear together, including my new shoes, and shove them in my sports bag. Luckily, Beth's mum has the dress back. I tell my mum I'm heading down to the leisure centre for some footie practise, and that I'll be going straight on to Beth's after. Beth and I have arranged to meet Jamie (and Adam) at the ball – I was amazed Mum didn't insist I had to go *with* Jamie but I'm glad – we want to give Jamie and Adam the biggest shock possible! I hardly mention the big event to Mum but, before I get to the front door, she corners me and manages to tell me another seventy things I can't do. By the time she's finished I think we've both completely forgotten it's supposed be fun. It's more like some ordeal, full of deadly hazards that I'll be lucky to come away from alive: Don'tdrinkanythingthatyouhaven'tseenpouredyourselfandif youdodrinkalcoholonlyhaveonedon'thaveanythingtodowith anyoneiftheyofferyoutabletsorfunnyciggiesoranythingelsenev erbealonewithoneboystickclosetoBethandJamieatalltimes;ify ouwanttocomehomejustringandwe'llcomeandcollectyoustrai ghtawayandifyouaretheretilllatedon'tacceptaliftwithanyonea partfromyourfatherorBeth'sfather . . . and so on and so on and so on.

Deep Thought for the Day

I'm beginning to work out why so many kids get into deep trouble, especially if their parents go on anything like mine do all the time. They not only put ideas into our heads that weren't even there in the first place but there's a fair chance the kids'll go for it just to prove they've got a mind of their own. How weird is that?

If Beth's mum is anything like as good at doing make-up as her auntie is at dressmaking, I might look passable. Her auntie's really done the biz with Gran's dress and it fits like it was made for me. Talk about slinky – I've seen snakes with looser skins. Unfortunately, most of the snakes I know don't tend to wear bras and knickers, and I really started to worry what underwear would fit underneath, but Beth's mum said she could easily sort it out for me later. As I can't imagine the full effect until the rest's done, I change back into my T-shirt and jeans.

Beth's mum's finally ready. She's got all the make-up stuff down from the attic and laid it all out on the kitchen table. Beth and I are both gobsmacked at just how much there is and that it's never even been opened. There are even things that Beth's mum can't remember what they were for. If *we* weren't going to use them, she says, we could probably open a make-up shop.

She starts with our hair. I'd already trawled through a whole pile of magazines looking for something that I like (and that I've got enough hair for). Strangely enough, the one we all agreed on, from the ones I'd torn out, was a photo of this model called Twiggy taken in the Sixties and we all also agreed that her face wasn't unlike mine (except she was blonde).

First we both have to go and wash our hair. My hair's dead straight, so Beth's mum does a sort of page-boy cut (I think that's what they call it); quite short at the back, but with one side slightly longer than the other. Every ten seconds I ask Beth if it's still OK, until the poor thing's nodding like one of those stupid toy dogs you see in the backs of cars. Instead of a fringe, her mum cuts it so that one side almost covers my left eye. A bit annoying, but I reckon it makes me look a bit mysterious – well, as mysterious as I could ever be. I also like it because I can hide behind it. Beth's mum eventually says she's finished and after she's given it a good blow-dry, she hands me the mirror (Beth tells me later I actually gasped). I look just like the girl in the picture. Cool, or what?

'What a clever mum you've got, Beth,' I say, so her mum can hear. 'Thanks ever so.'

Beth usually wears her thick hair tied back, but we all agree, like the girls in the dress shop suggested, that she should wear it up, to give her more height. All it really needs is trimming (like a hedge or a scruffy dog, I say). By the time her mum's finished, Beth looks like one of those girls in a James Bond film – all sort of slinky and quite grown-up-looking with a few wispy bits hanging down at the sides. Dead sexy.

Time for the make-up. First of all Beth's mum scrubs both our faces with this stuff we'd never heard of called cold cleansing cream and we're both gobsmacked at how grubby the cotton wool looks after she's done it.

'We must have been walking around with filthy expressions for years,' Beth giggles.

Then her mum does colour tests to find the right foundation. That's what goes on underneath the make-up, apparently. She says that being so young we'd hardly need any. As I'm all healthy looking with rosy cheeks, she decides that I need a little bit to stop me looking like a tractor driver on her night off, or that awful pink-faced gardening woman off the telly who my dad fancies. The foundation suggested for me, when she takes the lid off, is bright green and Beth and I both stare at it in horror, thinking I'll end up like the Wicked Witch of the East. Beth's mum says it takes away the rosiness. Beth, whose skin is coffee-coloured and not at all blotchy, hardly needs anything at all.

Then, with a great big brush, Beth's mum shoves on this ever-so-faint dark shadow under my cheekbones – to make them stand out, she says. All the time she keeps telling us to remember that less-is-more when we do our own make-up and that if we overdo it, we'll end up looking like Widow Twanky out of some naff old panto.

Beth and I watch with our eyes wide. It's like viewing a real live artist at work. When Beth's mum finishes the first bit, and before we can say anything, she suddenly wipes off what she's done and makes us do it all again ourselves. At first I'm all fingers and thumbs and come out looking like one of those white-faced clowns who's just had an accident, but after a couple of tries I get the hang of it pretty well. Beth's a natural from the start – it's obviously in the genes.

When she's done both of our faces, Beth's mum makes us write down all the stuff she's used so that we'll be able to do it again on our own. This is the bit Beth's mum says she really likes. She's like an artist preparing a canvas before the real work begins. I can tell she's in her element and loving every second.

It's time for our eyes and eyebrows. She tells us that to have cool eyebrows they have to be trained – a bit like rose bushes, and she shows us how to brush and pluck them, following the direction they grow naturally. Mine are quite dense and there are a few thick hairs which have strayed from the rest and are sitting defiantly in the middle just above my nose. Beth's mum sets about them with tweezers until I'm nearly blubbing.

'The things you have to go through to be beautiful,' I moan.

'If you want to make it easier,' she says, 'you should pluck them every week.'

Sod that, I say to myself.

She ends up by going over mine with eyebrow pencil to make them stand out. As Beth's eyebrows are jet black, they don't need it.

By the time she gets to my eyes I've forgotten the pain. My eyes are fairly big, Beth's mum says, so she decides that we can try a quite heavy eyeshadow. She asks me if I mind, but I say I don't care any more. It's funny, it's as if the face she's working on isn't mine anyway. She chooses a dark sort of purply-grey colour and sets about doing my eyelids with one of the millions of little brushes she has in her kit. Beth's eyes are slightly smaller than mine, so her mum tries a colour lighter than her skin tone, with a bit of sparkle in to make them stand out more. Cool? Not half! They end up looking absolutely wicked. By this time we're both getting quite het up and can't wait to see the final effect. But Beth's mum still has to show us how to do the eyeliner and mascara bit and then makes us do it ourselves. We both find that we're better at doing each other's make-up so have to swear never to be far away when either of us is going out. Whether this will work for the rest of our lives, who knows? We might have to marry the same bloke.

Yippee, it's time for lippy! Beth's mum tries lots before we all decide on a strong, dark, almost plum colour for me while Beth goes straight for one which matches her dress – flame-red and slightly glossy. Her mum makes us do it again ourselves after she's shown us how. It takes us ages to get used to using a brush, but we both agree the finished effect's much better than just plastering it on with a lipstick. Lastly, she puts a lip-liner on mine, ever so slightly around the edge, to make my lips look bigger and then does exactly the opposite with Beth's. I can't help wondering what the guys in my football team would say if they could see all this palaver.

By the time we get to have a look at ourselves in the dining room mirror, we've both been so caught up with the individual bits that we're completely shocked when we see the whole caboodle. Beth looks like something straight out of a movie – completely gorgeous, but, because she's pretty anyway, I'm not really that surprised. Me? That's a different story. We all agree I'm completely unrecognisable. I keep gawping at the mirror, trying to remember what I used to look like. It's funny, although it appears that I've not got very much make-up on, my whole face has been sort of transformed. Beth's mum sits back proudly and smiles widely as if to say, See, the old girl ain't lost it yet.

'Hey, Ell,' says Beth, in a hushed voice, 'you look about twenty. I've never seen anything like it. Go and put the dress on, quick.'

I slip into Gran's dress and climb into my new shoes. Beth does the same and together we half run and half stumble up the stairs to her parents' bedroom where there's a proper full-length mirror. Because the dress is so skin-tight I decide I can't wear a bra and as I rush up the stairs I can feel my boobs jiggling. Hey-ho! When I look at myself in the mirror, it almost frightens me. It isn't me . . . is it? It's someone completely different. Gran's dress makes me look like someone straight out of the pages of a fashion magazine, and as I stand there, I find myself striking model-type poses. Everything's perfect apart from that dratted knicker line. Luckily Beth's mum has got a short black slip to wear underneath my dress, otherwise I'd have had to go without any knickers at all.

At that moment Beth's dad arrives home looking knackered. He had an emergency at the hospital and had to do an operation. Beth's mum kisses him and tells him to wait at the bottom of the stairs and then yells for both of us to come down. We stop at the top of the stairs and do one of those head-over-one-shoulder pouty stares, just like we've seen models do. It's weird, we hadn't rehearsed it.

Beth's dad looks like he's seen a ghost.

'Who the . . . ? Is that . . . ?' he exclaims, genuinely shocked. 'I don't believe it – and my little Beth. You look sensational – both of you. I can't believe you're the same girls.'

He turns to his wife.

'What have you done to them, darling? I knew you were

good, but not that good. If I was thirty years younger I don't know what I'd think. I tell you what, I just pity any other girls at that ball.' He turns away, and as he does so, I notice he has tears in his eyes.

We both saunter down the stairs as elegantly as possible in our new shoes and twirl around in front of Beth's mum and dad who can only laugh with a mixture of pride and disbelief.

It's now about six . . . only one hour to go. Beth and I are out in her back garden having our pictures taken by her dad. He's a right gadget freak it turns out, so he's got the very latest digital camera. When he's done, we all troop back indoors for a cup of tea while he up loads them into the computer.

Ten minutes later, he comes down and places the print-outs proudly on the kitchen table. I tell you, if seeing myself in the mirror was weird, the photos were even weirder. Beth and I just stand giggling at what looks like two proper, sophisticated, grown-up women.

'Jeez, Beth,' I say quietly, 'that dress makes you look so slim.'

'What d'you mean – makes me *look* slim?'

'Hang on, don't get in a strop, you know what I mean. I bet you've never seen yourself like that before. You're flipping gorgeous.'

'What about you? You could be a proper fashion model looking like that – couldn't she, Mum?'

Beth's mum looks down at the pictures and sighs.

'The thing is Ella, darling, you do have the perfect figure, the perfect height and the perfect face for the business. The right people could make you into anything they want. You've got the kind of face that lends itself to all sorts of styles – it's just what the designers and photographers like. They can't really use pretty-pretty, it's too specific. Have you ever thought of doing it?'

'Doing what, sorry?'

'Being a model.'

I glance back at the pictures and then back at Beth's mum. For once, I'm lost for words. What was she saying? Was she joking? I feel so mixed-up. I've never even thought of myself as particularly attractive, let alone anything else. I knew I wasn't necessarily ugly, but that was about it. The first time a boy has ever noticed me in that way was on the footie pitch that time and that was only because of my boobs.

It's time for Beth's dad to take us to the town hall. I feel a bit like a bride must do being led down the aisle. We've arranged to meet Jamie and Adam at the entrance. Gran's given me this small, shiny black beaded evening bag to match my dress, and Beth's mum puts together a little touch-up kit in case we smudge ourselves. I agree to carry it for both of us.

The Belles of the Ball

Sitting in the back of a huge, lush Merc, dressed up like a film star, with Beth's dad driving us like a chauffeur, is just about as off-the-wall as anything I've ever done!

At the town hall steps, there's a man in a long coat and top hat, whose job it is to open car doors. Luckily he's got a big umbrella, because it's started peeing down. As soon as they see us, the photographers from the local papers rush forward and start snapping away like we really *are* important. A girl asks for our names, and Beth realises it's the same reporter who came to see her about the boot sale. She obviously doesn't recognise us – why would she? I don't. Beth nudges me and speaks to her in her poshest voice.

'I'm Bethany de Francesca and this my friend, Ellesandra Somerville-Clarke.'

'Are you mad?' I whisper, hardly able to stop giggling. 'Why did you say that?'

'I dunno. I just felt like it. It's brilliant, if we do get into trouble, they won't know it's us.'

In the huge entrance hall, there's a whole load of people milling about. Quite a lot of them turn round and start staring. It's as if we've walked in starkers. Oh damn, why, oh why, did I get myself into all this? In the distance, under a huge coat of arms thing, I can just make out Hannah wearing that terrible dress. She's just arrived with Adam's brother, Greg. My dear sister obviously doesn't recognise us, but Gorgeous Greg stares straight at us. I get so self-conscious, I have to look the other way. I spot a few girls who I know, in a huddle by the door, giggling excitedly. Then someone recognises Beth and the next minute they're all yapping away and pointing as if we've just caught fire. Where are Jamie and Adam, for God's sake?

Suddenly I hear this voice from behind.

'Ell, you look really wicked. I can hardly believe it's you.'

I turn round to see Adam, all dressed up in a suit and bow-tie and looking really fab.

'Hi, Adam,' I say with a giggle, 'that's because you're used to me looking like a scruffy old bag.'

'Don't go off on one again. Anyway, it's not. It's just that I didn't recognise you, until Jamie pointed you out. I was just gawping like everyone else.'

'Well, you look pretty cool too. I don't think I've ever seen you dressed up.'

'Take a look at your brother, then.'

'Where?'

'Over there, talking to Beth.'

I swivel round and see Jamie wearing the wickedest black suit I've ever seen. He hired it especially for tonight. Beth and Jamie are about the most glamorous-looking people in the room. I wish I could enjoy it like Beth seems to.

'Anyway, I wasn't sure you were still talking to me,' I say.

'Me neither. You look far too grand to want talk to me.'

'You should've seen what we went through to get like this. It's all down to Beth's mum.'

'I thought you looked OK before, but this is something else. It's a bit scary.'

93

I can't believe he just said that and I only just manage to reply, 'It's still boring old me underneath.'

'I never think you're boring, Ell – a bit pissy sometimes, but not . . .'

'I don't mean it, Adam, honest. I'm really sorry about what I said the other week.'

'Me, too. Look, I'm crap at dancing, but it'd be a real laugh to walk into the main room with you looking like this. Someone said The Fugitives are just about to go on.'

I must be an inch or so taller than Adam owing to the heels I'm wearing, but I'm feeling really excited that he's my mate again. As I walk through the crowd, trying not to wobble, I suddenly feel really stupid. Wearing a dress like this that shows off every bit of my body makes me feel really shy. Worse still, practically every bloke we pass, looks me up and down like if I'm some sort of exhibition piece. I even have to check my slip hasn't dropped below my hemline.

I put my arm through Adam's, in a way to tell everyone I'm with him, and I feel him go all tense. At the far end of the entrance hall we're about to walk past where Greg and my sister are standing with a few other giggly hangers-on. I've never been this close to Adam's brother before and realise just how good-looking he really is – ten out of ten in fact. He looks even taller and more rugged close up. He breaks away slightly from his crowd when he works out that it's his younger brother with me.

Suddenly, as if she's just seen the light, Hannah sees it's me too and her mouth literally falls open like Beth's dad's did. She stares at my dress in disbelief.

94

'Ella?' she squeals, with a hint of panic in her voice.

'Hi, Han,' I call back – all cool-like.

'Where did you get that amazing dress?'

'Off Gran.'

'But it's . . . it's fabulous. Why didn't you tell me about it?'

'I did – you had a go at me, remember. You told me not to come dressed as a granny. Anyway, you weren't there when she gave it to me.'

'And who cut your hair and . . .?'

'Sorry, Hannah, aren't you going to introduce me?'

She whirls round and it's Gorgeous Greg, cutting right across her as she speaks.

'Oh, sorry, Greg, this is my sister, Ella.'

'Sister?' he says, looking me up and down. He stops at my chest. Oh God, I knew I should have worn a bra. 'I didn't know you had a sister. Let alone a beautiful one.'

Hannah tries to hide her disapproval and I try not to giggle or go red.

'Oh well, I didn't think it . . .'

Greg completely talks over her again.

'Ella, that's a lovely name. I'm Greg, Adam's brother.'

'I-er-know,' I say, completely tongue-tied. I feel such an idiot.

'What do you do?' he asks.

What do I do? What does he think I do? Then I suddenly realise he thinks I'm older than Hannah. Oh my God!

Adam and I start giggling. If only Greg could have seen me on Friday, on the way back from school, in my yucky uniform. Adam jumps in and saves me.

'Sorry Greg – can't hang around. We want to catch The Fugitives. They're just kicking off.'

Gorgeous Greg, who's now got his back to my sister, holds out his hand to take mine. How grown-up is that? (And how shy am I turning out to be?) Hannah's looking at me as if she could tear my liver out and stuff it down my own swan-like throat. Greg's blue eyes are boring straight into mine as I'm practically the same height as him now and I start feeling shaky at the knees. God, I hope I don't wet myself.

'Well, I'm very pleased to meet you Ella,' he says in his soft, rather posh voice, bowing ever so slightly. 'I do hope we meet again later.'

The Fugitives are cool. I've seen them a couple of times before and have both their CDs so I know practically all the words. Adam and I pick our way across the floor to where Beth and Jamie are leaping about like mad things. Long slinky dresses and high-heeled shoes are all right for posing in, but crap for dancing – especially the way I dance (arms and legs all over the place stylie). My get-up, thankfully, forces me to just stand there wiggling my bum which, quite a bit later, as I was told by Adam, looked quite sexy. While the band is taking a break, Sarah Smith runs over. She's in our class and although a bit of a know-all, is quite nice all things considered. I'm surprised to see she's with another couple of girls from our year.

'Ella, it *is* you, isn't it! You look amaaaaazing! We all thought you must be another older sister of yours that we didn't know about. When you first came in, we just about recognised Beth, but we couldn't work out who you were.'

She waves and beckons to the others.

'Where did you go to have all this done? It must have cost a fortune.'

I could tell a huge lie but decide not to.

'It was Beth's mum,' I confess. 'She used to do it for a living.'

I must say I'm beginning to feel a bit fed up with all this attention. I wonder if this is what it's like to be famous? If it is, I reckon it would drive me bonkers after a while. Beth seems to be loving it, of course, but she always was more of a show-off than me.

When the band finishes their first set, a rather hot and sweaty Jamie comes over and says that we could go to the VIP lounge for a drink and something to eat if we want. Poor Adam looks really miserable because he hasn't got a VIP ticket, but Jamie asks one of the organisers on the front desk if we could take a special guest and he says yes. As we approach the two girls checking passes to the VIP lounge, I look back over my shoulder and see Hannah, still staring at me in disbelief. I'd practically ordered Mum and Dad not to tell her that I'd been invited to the VIP lounge, but quite frankly Hannah is usually so up her own you-know-what that she wouldn't have remembered if they had told her.

'Flipping hell, this as a bit posh,' says Beth in a low voice.

I look round the huge room watching the waiters, darting in and out of the smart guests, with silly little snacks on plates. Canapés, Adam says they're called.

'They're all staring at us again,' I whisper to Beth.

'I know, I keep having to check that my boobs haven't escaped.'

'Would the ladies like a champagne cocktail?'

I turn round and notice one of the waiters is talking to us. He obviously thinks we must be old enough to drink because of the way we look.

'Don't mind if I do,' I say, as the others lunge for his tray.

If there really is a God, then he must be out the back mixing the flipping drinks. All of us agree that these champagne cocktail thingies are fantastic. They've even got little raspberries on sticks in them – how cool's that?

'Jeez,' said Jamie, 'they're a bit strong, aren't they?'

'Good job they don't do it in pints,' giggles Adam. 'We'd be legless.'

Then this guy called Derek Something-or-other comes over and asks if we're the young people who gave such a generous donation. He'd been expecting us, apparently. It turns out he was the one who wrote the thank-you letter to Dad. We nod our heads nervously, but all he does is lead us over to shake hands with the mayor, our local MP, some old lady who, I find out later, practically owns Rainsfield and a bunch of other posh-looking people.

'This must be what it's like being the Queen,' I whisper to Adam.

'I feel like one in this outfit,' he whispers back.

Suddenly I notice HIM!

Lounging on a big sofa with a few of his mates, as out of place as we must look and just like he is in his pictures, it's him – Will Bradley – in a shimmering electric-blue suit and black Raybans. He really is about as cool as it's possible to look while still being on the planet. Just as I'm staring, he glances across to me and Beth and mutters something to his mates. They all laugh.

Beth catches them laughing too.

'What do you reckon he said? I bet it was something to do with my boobs.'

'I dunno,' I answer, 'but he was taking the piss out of one of us.'

I still can't get used to all this attention. If only they knew who I really was underneath, I might be able to feel less self-conscious.

'Hang on,' says Beth. 'Oh my God, I think they're coming over!'

'Oh, damn! What are we going to do?' I almost shout.

'Hi there,' says Will Bradley, 'I'm Will and these three ugly dudes are in my band. This is Spike and this is Jake and this is Delaney. Guy's gone off chasing some chick. Would you like to join us?'

'Hello,' says Beth, in a slightly faltering voice. I try to speak but nothing really comes out. I must not giggle. I must not giggle.

'Sure,' I say, in a bit of a daze. 'Come on,' I say to the others.

They smile at Beth and me, but Jamie and Adam are left standing awkwardly, not knowing what to do.

'Can't we ditch the kids?' says Spike to Will as we walk over to their table. It takes me a while to realise they're talking about Jamie and Adam.

Beth and I stand there like lemons, not having a clue what to say. I just don't know what to do with my arms and legs – it feels like these blokes seem to be undressing me with their eyes. I bet they wouldn't even bother if I were in my normal clothes.

'So what are you two called?' asks Will, speaking to Beth and me.

Beth and I hesitate, both wondering whether we should pretend to be the people Beth said we were at the door, or ourselves. The trouble is I can't remember who I'm supposed to be.

'C'mon, it can't be that difficult,' says Jake.

Beth and I look at each other and start giggling. How pathetic that must look.

'I didn't realise I said something funny,' says Will. 'I only asked your names.'

Beth and I now have a proper fit of the giggles, probably because we're so nervous. At this point Jamie and Adam come over and obviously think we're laughing at something the band has said.

Beth manages to get her voice back.

'My name's Beth and this is Ella . . . oh yes, and this is Jamie and Adam.'

None of the four guys even turns round to look at Jamie and Adam. I'm not sure, but I'm starting to wonder whether they're beginning to realise how old we are.

'Do you both work round here?' asks Will.

Oh no, it's happening again. I look at Beth and she looks at me. Then we both look over to Adam and Jamie, and all four of us start laughing.

'Have you been drinking a lot of that stuff?' Spike asks, sounding a bit annoyed.

Why does everything sound really funny when you've got the giggles? I can't believe it, here's my big chance to get to know Will Bradley, and I'm acting like a right idiot.

'We're all still at school,' says Adam.

The guys look round at him like he's something our cat's dragged in, and then back to Beth and me.

'How old are you two?' asks Will, frowning.

'How old do you want us to be?' I reply, getting back a bit of my composure.

'Older than those two blokes, I hope,' he says quietly. 'Anyway, what are they hanging around for? A Coke and a packet of crisps?'

'We actually came with them,' Beth says bravely.

'Well, you're with us now – tell them to piss off.'

Adam hears this and walks over and stands right in front of Will Bradley.

'Has that crap music you play made you deaf? Ella and Beth are with us tonight – OK?'

There is a stunned silence as we all stare at Adam. The four musicians look at each other in astonishment, as if to say, 'Shall we take them now?' But even they must realise a fight in a place like this would do them no good at all, especially with all the press around.

'You don't know how lucky you are we're not outside, sonny,' says Will Bradley in a horrid sneering voice. 'You'd be going home in an ambulance. Anyway, isn't it getting near you and your mate's bedtime?'

Suddenly I have to say something. I can't let him get away with that.

'There's no need to be so rude. They've done nothing to you. Leave us alone.'

The band sidles off, trying to look cool and muttering stuff like 'jailbait' and 'school kids', but we all look at each other and start laughing again.

'Do you want to buy my two Will Bradley CDs?' I whisper to Adam. 'I brought them for him to sign.'

'Ooh, yes please,' says Adam, 'then I can ask him if he'll allow me to shove them up his arse.'

I fall about laughing again and realise I really do like him.

Gorgeous Greg

Deep Thought for the Day

Isn't it weird? You can do your head in about someone for ever, lust over their pictures on your bedroom walls, dream of meeting them and go over and over what you'd say if you ever did, and then . . . and then, in about two seconds flat, the whole dream goes belly-up and you think the subject of your devotion is a bit of a creep. Life, eh!

I wonder if all famous people turn out like Will Bradley. Maybe thinking you can have any girl you want, whenever you want, has made him the creepster that he is today. I suppose he's just got used to clicking his fingers and expecting us to come running. Maybe that's what being famous is all about. Because we make such a fuss of them, they can never live up to what we imagine they're like. It's like making a meal with all your best things, roast chicken and chocolate chip ice cream all on one plate. It would probably make you throw up, because those flavours don't go together.

The funny thing is, I do feel a bit sad – like I've lost something precious.

Back to the ball. The four of us – Beth, Jamie, Adam and I – eventually leave the VIP lounge, having had another one of those wicked cocktails (sorry, Mum!) and head back to the main hall where stupid Will Bradley and his stupid band are just about to kick off. He struts out to the front of the stage, does that one-two-three thing with the microphone (that the sound-man's bound to have done already) and then gives the broad Will Bradley smile that we all know (and *used* to love). Just as he's about to sing, he sees us lot in the audience halfway back. Beth and me wave and he looks the other way quickly.

He might be a prat, but he's still bloody good on stage and after a couple of songs I almost forget what went on in the VIP lounge. But I'll soon remember again after all this is over. I can already see a few gaps appearing on my bedroom wall.

Every time the music stops, someone comes up to me and tries to chat me up. Adam gets more and more annoyed until, eventually, he plucks up the courage and slips his arm round me, like I'm *his*. I can feel his hand hot through the thin material of Gran's frock and suddenly I want to snog him like crazy. Maybe being dressed up isn't so bad after all. The trouble is, as soon as he realises that I've realised what he's doing, he whips his arm away again.

I drag Beth off to the ladies for a conference.

'Hell, Beth, I don't know if I can handle this much longer. What am I supposed to do now? Adam seems so scared of me!'

'Whatever it is, don't do it on the dance floor,' she giggles. 'It'll scare him off completely.'

'How are you getting on?' I ask.

'Don't ask. It's driving me mad too. He's such a bloody gentleman, your brother. I reckon if anything's ever going to happen I'll have to do it myself.'

It's funny, but it makes me feel a bit weird thinking of my best friend and my brother getting together. I suppose it's something you get used to.

Moving so we're under the light, we touch up each other's make-up, not trusting to do our own ourselves (especially with my shaky hands).

The ball is obviously a huge success, but the time seems to go too fast. I catch a glimpse of the big clock out of the corner of my eye and see that it hit midnight some time ago. I grab the others and rush to the entrance hall. I look round desperately, but can't see my dad anywhere. Oh my God, don't say he's come and gone off in a huff because we weren't ready and waiting. I'll never be allowed out again – ever. Just as Adam and Jamie go off to the gents, I feel a tap on my shoulder – oh my God, it's Gorgeous Greg again.

'Ah, Ella, I hoped I'd run into you before the end. Have you had a good time with my little brother?'

He really is gorgeous, I think to myself, but thank God I realise I fancy Adam far more.

'Fab, thanks,' I say, looking over his shoulder for my dad. 'I've never been to anything like this before.'

Doh! As soon as I've said it, I want to kick myself. How uncool must that sound on a scale of one to ten?

'I go to quite a few. Perhaps I'd enjoy it more if you'd come with me sometime?'

I'm just wondering what to say next, when I see Hannah coming towards us through the crowd. She's obviously seen Greg chatting me up again. Oddly enough, she doesn't look angry with me, but more with him.

'Oh hi, Han,' I say rather coyly.

'Still here, Ella? I'm surprised you haven't turned into a

pumpkin. I thought you had to go home at twelve – it's nearly twenty past. You never know what might happen if you hang around here too long.' With that she glared at Greg as if she wanted to kill him

I smile weakly but decide that the comment wasn't really meant for me, so hold my tongue. Just then I spot Dad, nervously trawling his eyes round all the girls, trying to spot me. The poor old fella goes past me about three times. Eventually he makes his way across the room presumably to ask Hannah if she's seen me.

'Hi Dad, I've been looking for you everywhere,' I say.

He stares at me for a split second and then his mouth falls open. I'm getting a bit used to this.

'Ella, darling! I can hardly recognise you. There I am, looking for my little daughter, and you're here all the time. I can't believe it. You look absolutely fabulous, darling, and so grown-up. Have you had a good time?'

'Fantastic thanks, Dad.'

'You look just like my mother when she was young – it's uncanny. We must get a photo. Is this Beth's mother's handiwork?'

'Hello, Mr Furgusson,' says Beth, who has just joined us with Adam and Jamie.

'Beth – you too! You look simply wonderful.'

'A bit hot and sweaty, I'm afraid.'

I introduce Adam to Dad and Dad looks rather relieved. Probably because we don't seem too drunk. Luckily, we all had plenty of water after the cocktails, so the effects have more or less worn off.

106

'Are you and Beth ready? Your mother said you might like to sleep over, Beth, so she dropped off some things for you. Do you want a lift, Adam? I reckon I can squeeze you in.'

And squeeze us in he did. Jamie, typically, dives in the front with Dad – much to Beth's distress, while the rest of us are crammed into the back of Mum's little car. If I was any closer to Adam they'd have to use a crowbar to prise us apart. I can even feel the heat from his body and his heart bumping away. I decide there's never going to be a time like this again. Making well sure Dad's not looking in the rear-view mirror, I turn and give him a big kiss on the cheek. Beth sees me do it and starts giggling.

When we get home, Mum's still up. Beth and I walk into the kitchen and Mum, who's having a hot drink, practically chokes when she sees us.

'Ella, darling, and you, Beth! I can hardly believe it. You both look so grown-up.'

'I keep telling you I don't need my nappy changed any more, Mummy,' I say cheekily.

'I wouldn't have believed it if I hadn't seen it with my own eyes. Did you have a lovely time? I hope you didn't do . . .'

'Mum, please don't start the inquisition. We're both knack – worn out. Could we just have a cup of tea? I promise I'll tell you all about the dreadful things we got up to tomorrow.'

'Flipping hell!'

'Flipping hell!'

It's one-thirty and Beth and I have just staggered up to my room and flopped on the bed. My feet feel as if someone's just used them for a marathon.

'What was that all about?' I half say, half groan.

'Search me, I'm still in shock.'

'I don't reckon I'll believe tonight really happened when I wake up. *If* I ever wake up.'

Beth seems in a sort of a daze.

'I'm not sure it did. We can't really have told Will Bradley to sod off?'

'Wasn't Adam cool?' I say.

'And the girls from our year really didn't recognise us?'

'And . . .'

'And was Gorgeous Greg really trying to pull you?'

'Did you see all that?' I say. 'I was beginning to think I'd made it up.'

'He was all over you. Does he know how old you are?'

'You can bet Han's told him. She was going off her trolley.'

'What are you going to do?'

'About what?'

'Greg.'

'Nothing, I prefer his brother – you know that. Anyway, he probably sleeps with all his girlfriends on the first date.'

'So?'

'Beth! Are you mad?'

'Well, we've gotta start some time. It might as well be with someone who knows his way around. I could wait for your brother till I'm a geri-bloody-atric.'

'Beth! You're seriously not serious, are you?'

'Oh I don't know. I'm just glad it wasn't me Greg was after. I'd have probably gone home with him.'

'Beth! Shut it! Mum and Dad might hear.'

'At least you managed to kiss Adam.'

'Yeah, only on the cheek, but I think I might have scared him stiff.'

'Stiff?' Beth says with a giggle.

'You know what I mean,' I say. 'Oh well, with a bit of luck it might give my big brother ideas. You never know.'

'I hope so. I'm going to burst if something doesn't happen soon. He looked so fit tonight.'

'So did you.'

'I looked as good as it gets, I admit, but what about you? Even me, your best mate, could hardly believe it. How do you feel now it's over?'

'It was all a bit weird. I'm trying to get my head round it. It was as if I'd gone out in the wrong body sort of thing – like I'd nicked someone else's.'

'I know what you mean. When I saw us in the lav mirror, I suddenly felt all strange. It was like a sort of horror film where aliens take over your body – only this time we were the aliens.'

'It seems like just about everything to do with pulling blokes is about how you look.'

'You're not wrong. It wouldn't need a survey to work that out. Just ask us.'

'I've never felt all girly like that before.'

Beth looked almost sad.

'And I forgot I was fat for a night.'

'Beth! Please, babe! You've got to stop this. You looked lush. There wasn't a bloke there who wasn't staring at you.'

'My boobs, more like.'

'Look, if you won't believe anything I'm saying, then just believe *that*. If you've got 'em, use 'em, I say.'

'It's going to be a bit funny being us again tomorrow.'

'I feel almost us again now. I'm not sure that I'd quite know how to carry on being her.'

'Her?' asks Beth.

'The girl I went to the ball as.'

'Yeah – I know what you mean. What do girls like that have for breakfast?'

'They're probably too busy doing their make-up,' I say gloomily. 'When do you think we'll do it again?'

Beth goes quiet for a second.

'I almost want to do it tomorrow, just to make sure.'

'Make sure?'

'That it really happened. Haven't you ever had one of those dreams where you do stuff you wouldn't normally?'

'Like snogging and stuff?' I say.

'Yeah. Hey, I've just had a thought. We could creep out at night as those other girls.'

'And we could have sophisticated lovers in gorgeous flats, who take us out to posh dinners and theatres and stuff,' I say, and lie back on the bed, staring dreamily at the ceiling.

'And we could make passionate love with them, before catching the bus home.'

'Hang on,' I say. 'They can bloody pay for cabs.'

'No one would ever know it was us. We could use those daft names I gave us at the main entrance to the ball.'

'I'd forgotten about them.'

'And I can't even remember what I said. I made them up on the spot.'

'I was Ellesandra Somerville something.'

'Oh yeah, and I was Bethany de someone. How cool is that?'

'I've just thought. What if they print our pictures in the paper?'

'They won't, will they?'

We talk away for about another half-hour before falling asleep, still in our make-up.

In the Cold, Cold Light of Day

It's eleven o'clock on Sunday morning and I've only just woken up. Beth's still flat out in a little ball beside me. I think I might just be having the first hangover in my life because my mouth tastes like a bear's pants and the twittering of the stupid birds outside is making my brain ache (don't *they* ever lie in?). I peer wearily round the room, only to see Gran's beautiful dress in a heap on the floor with my shoes and everything else. I almost want to say sorry to it, like it's injured or something. I hang it up gently, go for a wee and totter downstairs. Mum and Dad have gone out to a garden centre, it turns out, but Hannah's in the kitchen, staring into her Coco Pops like she could murder someone.

'Hi, Han, how are you feeling?'

No reply.

'Did you have a good time last night?'

No reply.

'What's up?'

'You've got a bloody nerve even asking, haven't you?'

'Sorry, have you got the hump with me or something?'

'I suppose you're really proud of yourself.'

'Sorry?' I say. 'I don't actually have a clue what you're going on about.' (I sort of do, but . . .)

'Oh, don't you?'

'Not till you let me in on it.'

'You mean you're telling me you weren't playing up to Greg?'

112

'I haven't told you anything yet. Anyway, it was him that was chatting me up, in case you didn't notice.'

'So what was all that shy little-girl-lost act all about then?'

'That was no act. I actually was dead shy if you must know. I've never been to anything like that before.'

'I bloody bet you haven't – not dressed like that.'

'Like what?'

'You know.'

'Look, Hannah – what's your problem? What has what I was wearing got to do with you or anyone else come to that?'

'Everything, especially if your boyfriend can't stop asking about your sister all the way home.'

'Look, I didn't know Greg was your boyfriend, and anyway, how do you make out that it was my fault?'

'Well, who else's could it have been?'

I see this is going nowhere, but keep on with it, because, if I walk away, it would be like saying I've done something wrong.

'If you want the truth, Beth and I were as gobsmacked by the way everyone went on as you were. I don't even know whether I liked it or hated it.'

'Hated it? I hope you're kidding. You were the centre of attention. And what about Beth, with her boobs hanging out all over the place?'

'You weren't exactly dressed like Mother Teresa.'

'At least I looked tasteful.'

'Tasteful? Yeah, I suppose you were, if you were going for the footballers' wives look.' God, did I really say that?

'So, what's the matter with that?'

'Well, if you don't know, I can't tell you.'

I feel myself revving up, but I'm determined not to have a proper fight.

'Anyway, Mum's going to have a word with you,' says Hannah, with a slight sneer.

'You what? About what? What have you said?'

'I just told the truth – that you were flirting with everyone and getting drunk and stuff.'

'That's a bloody lie and you know it. I reckon you're just jealous.'

'Jealous? Me? Of you? You've got to be out of your baby mind. How sad would that be? Jealous of my little sister.'

When Mum and Dad get home, I'm summoned into the living room. Mum starts the interrogation.

'We heard you had a good time last night.'

'Very, thanks,' I reply, guardedly.

'Hannah said you were flirting with all the boys and were a bit tipsy. She said she was embarrassed.'

'That's a bloo – flipping lie, Mum. I wouldn't know how to flirt.'

'That's what she said, anyway. I must admit I couldn't imagine you flirting.'

'It isn't true, that's why. It's so not fair! I couldn't help it if they kept coming up to me.'

'Maybe she was a little jealous?' Dad says with a sort of knowing look to Mum.

'Look, if you want to know how I behaved, just ask Jamie. He was with me practically all the time, except when I went to the loo.'

Mum's face begins to relax.

'Ella, I really don't approve of the drinking, as you know. You promised me you'd go easy. As for the rest, you certainly looked stunning – didn't she, Roy?'

Dad smiles and nods. 'You could hardly have blamed the boys for hanging around, that's for sure. Didn't Beth say her father took some pictures?'

I don't answer, because I'm beginning to lose my temper.

'Look, it's my turn to talk. I'm getting fed up with everyone treating me like a flipping kid, yeah? It's not fair. As it happened, I did have a couple of drinks that were a bit strong, but I realised it right away and stopped – and yeah, I was offered cigarettes and stuff, but I was having a perfectly OK time without any of that crap.'

Mum tries to butt in.

'There's no need to use bad . . .'

'Hang on a minute, why can't I finish? It's me that's being accused of stuff. The only reason I care what Hannah said is that it might make you stop me going to anything else.'

Just at that moment Hannah drifts in, still in her dressing gown and looking a right grumpster.

'Ah, Hannah,' I say, 'could you repeat what you told Mum and Dad about me?'

'Oh that. I've forgotten about it now.'

'Come on, Hannah,' I say. 'Say it again, if you dare.'

Hannah begins to look a bit like a rabbit caught in the headlights.

'I just said she was making a fool of herself, showing off and stuff.'

Mum looks at Dad again.

'Someone said you were really rude to Will Bradley,' says Hannah.

'Were you, Ella?' asks Dad

'If being rude to someone is staying with the boys that you're with and not going off with someone else, then maybe I was. They were really nasty, Dad.' I feel myself on the verge of blubbing, and turn to face the window.

'Well, it doesn't sound as if . . .'

'That's typical,' yells Hannah, 'you always take the side of Little Miss Perfect. I'm not listening to any more of this.'

At this precise moment, Beth strolls into the room, rubbing her eyes.

'Hi, everyone. Hi, Hannah, did you enjoy the thing last night?'

'You can shut up too,' yells Hannah and flies out of the room in tears.

'Was it something I said?' asks Beth, looking truly mystified.

Dad comes over and gives me a big hug.

'She'll be all right, I'll have a quick word with her. Then I've got to go,' he says. 'I'm playing golf with Mike in fifteen minutes. Can I give you a lift home, Beth?'

Beth and I give each other big hugs and then she goes off with Dad in the car.

Mum looks at me and for one second I think she's about to cry.

'So, darling, how was it really? Did you love being all dressed up?'

'I *think* I did. But I'm not sure. It was more of a shock than

116

anything else. It was all a bit sudden. I've never really thought about myself like that.'

'Your father and I were really shocked too. We just didn't realise how grown-up you could look.'

'It was pretty weird, Mum. Everyone kept staring. I felt a bit funny, almost like it wasn't really me in those clothes.'

'It just might be something you have to get used to.'

'But the real me likes playing football and making things and getting dirty and mucking about and stuff.'

'You can be both of those things, sweetheart. Just because you're sporty doesn't mean you can't look stunning now and again.'

'Then there's the Hannah thing,' I say gloomily.

There's a pause and then Mum says, 'I think you must try to understand her a little better. She's been obsessed by how she looks since she was a toddler and was used to getting all the attention. Then this Ella creature, who no one's even looked at before and who doesn't really care anyway, comes along and steals the show from right under her nose.'

'I just can't seem to do anything right in her eyes, Mum. If I knock around in my football kit she takes the mick and the minute I try something else she accuses me of showing off.'

'I suppose she was as shocked as the rest of us. You've always just been funny little Ella. I suppose because you never seemed that interested in what you looked like, we took you for granted. You never seemed to want new clothes and even when we did buy you things for birthdays or Christmas, we had to practically beg you to wear them.'

'I never thought anything really suited me.'

'This is probably why it's all such a shock now, darling. It just took Beth's mother and a beautiful dress. Anyway, I promise me and your dad won't treat you any differently.'

'And what about Hannah?'

'Just give her time. She really isn't a bad person underneath it all.'

Facing the Fans and Miss Braithwaite

Monday morning turned out to be quite an ordeal. When Beth and I got to school, the word had got round about Saturday night and how Beth and I were dressed up. This we could just about handle, but when the local newspaper came out the following day, everything went severely pear-shaped.

I walk into the classroom and there it is on Emma's desk, staring me in the face – or rather there *we* are, Beth and me, in full colour in the *Rainsfield Gazette*, sliding out of Beth's dad's Merc and looking like film stars going to a premier. The caption underneath reads: *Cinderellas at the Rainsfield Ball.*

Oh no, here we go again. I can feel myself going bright red, and then Becky Swithin starts reading it out loud in her poshest sing-song voice.

'Two glamorous young ladies added welcome sparkle to the already lavish proceedings at the Rainsfield Charity Ball on Saturday night. They gave their names to our reporters as Bethany de Francesca and Ellesandra Somerville-Clarke, but on checking the ticket stubs and the special guest list, no similar names were found. The mystery girls disappeared as enigmatically as they arrived, just after midnight . . . and our reporters remain at a loss as to their true identity.'

Becky's forced to stop for a second owing to the squeals of laughter from the others.

'What does "enigmatically" mean?' I ask, but Becky ignores me.

'I've already rung them,' she yells, leaping up and down like a mad thing. 'I left a message on their answering machine. We always get the newspaper first thing on Tuesday mornings.'

Beth, who'd read it before I arrived, looks across at me and I swear she's blushing for the very first time in her life.

'You idiot. What did you tell them?' I ask Becky angrily.

'I told them what they wanted to know. I'm not stupid.'

'What who wanted to know exactly?' comes a voice from behind me.

We all whip round, only to see that Her Royal Highness, Miss Braithwaite, has just bustled into the class.

'What's all the fuss about?' she continues, 'What have you got there, Beth?'

Beth, who I'd managed to slip the newspaper to, shoves it quickly under her bum and sits down firmly.

'I asked what you have there, Miss Middleton, that you so obviously don't want me to see.'

'Oh nothing, Miss.'

'Then you won't mind me seeing it, will you? Come along, hand it over at once.'

Beth slowly takes the newspaper from under her and hands it to Miss Braithwaite rather sheepishly. Miss B goes straight to the picture and then reads the caption underneath. After a few seconds, she looks up and her lizard-like eyes, magnified by her glasses, glance round the class, stopping at Beth again.

'This isn't you in this picture, is it?'

'Er . . . yes, Miss.'

'And you were masquerading as this Bethany de Francesca person.'

'Er . . . well, yes, Miss.'

'Why the ridiculous name?'

'I don't know, Miss – it just seemed a good idea at the time.'

It's a good job Beth's chest is covered up in the picture, I can't help thinking.

'Am I supposed to recognise your friend?' Miss Braithwaite continues.

A howl of laughter rocks the classroom. Poor Tilly looks as if she's going to wet herself and Donna McAllister starts to choke and rushes out of the room.

'I . . . er . . . don't know, Miss. You might have run into her.'

Miss B knows full well that Beth's my best friend and turns to peer at me through her thick lenses.

'It's not you, Ella Furgusson. It can't be. Is it?'

I stare at the floor, hoping it'll swallow me up.

'I asked if it was you Ella, or are you now – who does it say? – Ellesandra Somerville-Clarke these days?'

I can hardly hear myself speak over the other girls who are now cheering fit to burst. Mrs Rayburn, the head teacher, who must have been passing when Donna ran out of the class, looks through the window in the door to check if everything's all right.

'Er . . . yes, Miss,' I eventually get out.

'What have you done to yourself?'

121

'Nothing, Miss, it was just a bit of a laugh.'

Miss B, who has obviously never looked remotely glam in her life (let alone done anything for a bit of a laugh), gives me a really withering glare.

'I see. Well, I suppose I can't control what you children do at the weekends unfortunately, but while you are here, this is my domain, and I am in total command. Do you understand? Now put this thing away.'

I fully expect her to carry on trying to make us look stupid, but thankfully she just hands the newspaper back to Beth theatrically, as if she's handling the most disgusting porno magazine or one of those plastic bags you put dog poo in.

'Now class, if you're all quite ready, might I most humbly suggest we get down to some work, for that, believe it or not, is what you're here for, despite what others might think.'

She glares over her glasses at Beth and me, but I'm sure I detect a slight twinkle in her eye.

Deep Thought for the Day

Though Miss Braithwaite seems to really disapprove of Beth and me, I can't help thinking that underneath it all she rather likes us. Perhaps some of the things Beth and I do she'd really liked to have done herself.

By break time, just about the whole school has seen the picture, so when we go out into the yard we could be seventeen feet high and painted blue with yellow spots on and get less attention. Even the sixth-formers are staring, but I notice my sister, Hannah, and her mates are showing their backs to us in a really obvious way.

That afternoon, when I'm back home and sitting down to *The Simpsons*, Hannah walks in carrying two cups of tea. I haven't spoken to her since all that fuss yesterday.

'Look, Hannah,' I say, before she can get a word out. 'Don't go on at me again. I'm really sorry about Saturday night.' (I'm not really, but I've got to say something). 'I didn't mean anything, honest. It was all a laugh. Beth's mum used to work in fashion and she did our hair and make-up. We were as surprised as everyone else – honest.

Strangely enough, Hannah, for once, doesn't look miffed at all and just shrugs, hands me a cup, and then, out of the blue, puts her hand on my shoulder. How weird is that?

'I was going to talk to you, Ell. Look, if anyone should say sorry it's me. I think I went overboard saying all that stuff to Mum and Dad. I'm really sorry. You were right. It was Greg who was the prat. I never know where I stand with him. Just when I think I'm actually going out with him, he does something like that. The trouble is, he goes after anyone he hasn't had yet. It's a conquest thing. When you're like him, you have to keep reassuring yourself that everyone fancies you. It's dead weird, at one point I even felt sorry for you – like you needed looking after . . . that's when I wasn't wanting to strangle you. Do you know, when I saw the picture of you and Beth in the paper, I even felt a bit proud.'

'It won't happen again, Hannah, promise.'

'What? Are you mad, Ell? You looked great – really classy. I couldn't believe it was you. You're an absolute natural. It was so obvious, everyone thought so. We all said that whoever had done that to you and Beth was a genius. Look, does her mum still know anyone in that business? I'd love to work with models and make-up and stuff.'

That night I lie in bed thinking over and over about everything that has gone on in the last few days. One minute I'd been wondering if Adam fancied me or not and the next, his big brother, who most girls would pay money to go out with, made it pretty obvious that *he* did. But then it doesn't take a lot to realise that Greg didn't actually fancy the real me – fourteen-year-old Ella Furgusson from Year Nine, who plays in a boys' football team – but this strange person I'd turned up at the ball as. Then I realised that it took new hair, make-up and clothes to make boys fancy me and that made me a bit sad. Worse still, in a way, I realised that when I got over the embarrassment, I quite liked the attention. I even started worrying whether she (the girl I was at the ball) would gradually begin to take over my life and that the sort of mucking about, not taking anything too seriously, Ella, would eventually give up the fight. As it is, would boys now just want to go out with me because of the way I look, without even bothering to find out anything else? I'd seen girls like

124

Chloe Heath (dead pretty but full of herself) in the Sixth Form, turn into a sort of trophy for boys. I began to remember how some of the blokes looked at me at the ball, even proper men, all sort of serious – like – like you think they really fancied me and stuff. Wow! It's almost too much to get my brain around. Worst of all, I've hardly thought about football since Saturday morning – in fact even before then – and it's the thing I like most in the world.

Guess Who's Coming to Football?

What a weirdo weeko. I've hardly clapped eyes on Adam at all and I'm beginning to think he might have gone right off me again. I saw him at football practice on Wednesday evening, but he always seemed to be where I wasn't and vice versa. I've also texted him a couple times, but Jamie says he hardly ever reads his messages.

I keep looking at the photos of me and Beth that her dad took and wonder why I let myself look so ghastly the rest of the time. Dad once said that his car seems to go much better when it's clean and sparkly. Is that the same sort of thing (or am I finally going completely round the bend)? I've seen programmes about top models on the telly, and they seem to walk about looking really ordinary when they're not having their pictures taken. I suppose once you know you can do it, you don't have to try. Being beautiful when you want to be must be like something you carry in your handbag for emergencies. Wonder if I'll get like that one day?

Every time I see a mirror or catch myself in a shop window, I find myself walking like a model, swinging my hips and pouting and turning my head round before changing direction, like they do in fashion shows. Beth's worse. She keeps making out her school uniform's the big red dress and swirling round and round in strange places like the school bus stop or the lunch queue. How sad is that? The dinner ladies looked quite confused and our mates think we've gone slightly bonkers. Maybe they're right.

It's Saturday morning and I've just called round Beth's to go training.

'So what *are* you going to do about my brother?' I ask.

'Search me. Apart from snogging him to death, I haven't the foggiest. I don't have a clue how to start even.'

'Perhaps you should just launch in before he has a chance to run away.'

'You're a fine one to talk. You reckon you might've scared Adam off doing just that – and that was only a quickie on the cheek. Trouble is, I haven't a clue whether Jamie fancies the girl I was on Saturday night or just the plain, everyday, utility version.'

'I've been down that one too. I still think Adam stuck close to me that night because of how I looked and because he'd had a bit to drink. Maybe we should go halfway.'

'What, like try a bit harder the rest of the time.'

Beth looks a bit sad.

'But I haven't got any decent clothes.'

'Me neither,' I say, 'but maybe we could make them, or at least alter other things. I've been thinking about that quite a bit lately.'

'Do you know how?'

'No, but perhaps your auntie could teach us to sew after your mum's finished teaching us make-up. We could buy the stuff from charity shops and jumbles.'

'Whaa? Nobody goes to charity shops, it's so uncool.'

'They sometimes have really good things.'

'Well you won't catch me buying anything – no way.'

'Suit yourself, but will you come with me?'

'As long as no one sees us going in.'

'Let's look in that Oxfam shop on the way to the leisure centre. I've still got a bit of cash left from the great ball fund.'

There's a couple of charity shops in the High Street. We head into Help the Aged first, but, on this particular day, it looks like that's where the aged actually *get* their clothes. Oxfam had more stuff to choose from and I manage to find a couple of skirts and tops that hardly look as if they've been worn – and for practically nothing. I'm just under a size ten (but with slightly larger boobs and slightly narrower hips). One of the tops I find is really cool apart from a stupid glittery butterfly thingy on the front. I look at it closely and realise it can be unpicked quite easily. I hate things sewn or stuck on to clothes (always have) or T-shirts with slogans (yuck!). I think I must get it from my mum. Hannah has loads with stuff like 'Babe' and 'Sexy' written on the front. She even used to wear a necklace with her name in gold letters. How crap's that?

There's a little changing room at the back of the shop, and I'm in and out every few minutes. The only thing I disagree with Beth about is a tiny brown suede mini-skirt that's hanging on a rack all by itself in the cubicle, like it had been left by someone. Beth says that with my long legs I could get away with it, but I reckon I wouldn't even have the bottle to wear it out into the main bit of the shop.

'It might look a bit tarty if you wore it with heels,' she says, 'but if you had flatties, or trainers even, it would look cool. You could wear it with the black tights you've got on. Go on Ell, have a go?'

I put it on with a little short, blue, what-looked-like-lambswool jumper with a draw-string neck that I found in the kids section and come back out. The lady in the shop says she thinks it looks nice . . . so I buy it.

I manage to talk Beth into buying a few things. Beth always wants to wear black, because she says it makes her look slimmer. Sooner or later she's going to have to accept that she's a great shape now – I don't want her getting that stupid anorexia illness, where you can't bring yourself to eat and end up dead skinny – or dead dead.

Adam, it turns out, doesn't show up for football, which not only pisses me off, but makes me wonder if I really have scared him off for good. Apart from that, I'm really beginning to enjoy footie like I used to, now that the boys are treating me as one of them again. Beth seems to be throwing herself even more into the circuit training. It's as if what had happened at the weekend has spurred her into another gear, and I'm gobsmacked at how un-out of breath she is now. I even had difficulty keeping up – me! – Miss Fitness Features! Luckily after the training, our team has a practice match with the senior team and Beth goes home. She says she'll come back later when we've finished. We usually get massacred by the senior team and I'm expecting to have to do a lot of goalie work. Halfway through, it starts raining and the already soaking pitch turns into brown gravy with bits of grass sticking out of it. By the time I come off, I look like I've been in a mud-wrestling contest. I'm just making my way to the showers when I have the shock of my life. I hear this voice behind me.

'Excuse me, I'm looking for Ella Furgusson.'

I whip round only to see Gorgeous Greg Cresswell talking to the bunch of blokes behind me.

They point to me and all laugh real boy-laughs! It's as if they've sussed the plot already. If you could have seen Greg's face! The last time he'd seen me was dressed up to the nines, wearing full war paint and looking about twenty.

'Ella, is that you?' he asks, like he's seen a ghost (a muddy ghost, at that).

'Oh, er – yes. Hi! Sorry, I didn't expect to see . . . how did you know I was here?'

'I worked it out. My brother told me you went to the same leisure centre and that he usually goes on Saturdays. I didn't really expect you to . . .'

'Look like this?'

'Well, no. It's a bit of a shock.'

'Sorry,' I say feebly.

'It's just that I really enjoyed Saturday night.'

'Oh yeah, Saturday night.'

'No, I meant to say I enjoyed meeting *you*.'

Gosh, I suddenly feel a bit like I did then. I can feel myself slipping way out of my depth. He carries on in his smooth voice – the sort of voice that could charm the birds out of the trees, as Gran would say – or worse! Please don't giggle, Ella. It's weird, he talks as if he really knows me. I just keep staring, like I'm in a sort of trance.

'I wondered . . . maybe . . . sometime . . .?'

Suddenly my mind goes into overdrive. Perhaps Hannah hasn't told him how old I am. Surely he can't be asking a fourteen-year-old out . . . can he?

'I tell you what, why don't I ring you?' he says in the end.

I wait for him to ask for my number, but he doesn't seem to need it.

'Right, then,' I say.

'Right, then,' he says.

We stand looking at each other, like lemons, neither knowing what to say next. But I'm freezing my bits off and start to shiver.

'Sorry,' I say. 'Pneumonia alert. Got to have a hot shower – see you.'

I gallop off, leaving him standing like a punctured ball at a football match. As I'm running, I realise that I'm feeling relieved. It must be because the real me doesn't really want to go out with him.

After the shower, instead of putting on my old clothes, I decide to wear my new skirt and top. I look in the changing-room mirror and can hardly believe I'm wearing anything that short. Looks quite cool, though. Just as I've finished getting dressed my phone rings.

'Hi, Ell, it's me . . . Adam.'

Stay calm, Ell, stay calm!

'Oh, hi,' I say, as casual as I can. 'How you doing? I was giving up on you. I texted you twice.'

'Sorry, my charger's on the blink. I've had that sort of a week. Look, I really wanted to see you today, but I promised I'd do something for Greg. You know Greg – my brother.'

My mind races at a million miles an hour. Do I tell him I've just seen him, and that he tried to ask me out?

'Oh yeah, what?' I ask, trying to sound just polite.

'Oh, nothing. He's just about to buy this flash new car, and I promised to clean the old one because he thinks he's got someone coming round to look at it this evening. I'm broke and he's paying me way over the odds. I got Billy to stand in for me at footie. Oh, sorry, you must know that. What are you doing at the moment?' he asks.

'Not much, I've just finished football.'

'How did we do?'

'Bloody miracle. We drew. Everyone played great.'

'I bet it was because I wasn't there.'

'Rubbish, you're really good. We might have won if you'd been here.' (Flipping hell, listen to me paying compliments.)

'Oh yeah, me no think so,' he says.

'Why don't you come down here?'

'What, now? I thought you'd be off home.'

'Yeah, I would normally, but Beth and I were thinking of doing something after. My brother will probably be along.'

'I could be there in half an hour. Is that OK?'

As I switch off the phone, it suddenly dawns on me what a real creep Greg is. I mean, how tacky is that to try and pinch your brother's girlfriend? (If I *were* his girlfriend, that is.) And that's on top of trying it on at the ball when he was with my sister. And did he give Adam the job of cleaning his car so that he'll be out of the way when he wants to come and find me? Oh yes, and how did he know my number without me giving it to him? He's obviously pinched it off his brother. I could tell by the way that he was looking that he was only really interested in me because of how I was dressed at the ball. Then I get to thinking maybe he didn't pinch my number but decided that he wouldn't take it down because he couldn't take the risk of me turning up looking like I do normally. Either way, he's still a creep. Good-looking creep, though.

Beth was outside having a Coke with Jamie. When I told them about Greg and what I suspected he'd got Adam to do, they were as gobsmacked as me.

'What a slimy git,' said Jamie. 'You've got to tell Adam.'

'I thought about it, but then I thought I'd wait.' Wait, just to see if Adam wants to be my boyfriend, I think to myself.

'I reckon we could be cleverer than that,' says Beth. 'Like really embarrass the pants off the creep.'

'How?'

'Oh, I don't know. You could say you'll go on a date with him and turn up in your school uniform and no make-up or something. You could even paint some spots on – that'd be a right laugh.'

'Or your footie strip,' Jamie added.

'I don't think I'd dare.'

'You could dress up like you did for the ball again and then, when his tongue's hanging out, dump him halfway through the evening.'

'That'll involve seeing him again, though.'

'You've got to do something, Ell, if only for Adam's sake,' says Beth.

'Why not arrange to meet him somewhere and just not turn up?'

'I reckon I could manage that.'

Beth bursts out laughing.

'We could all walk past accidentally on purpose and ask who he's waiting for.'

'You're such a witch, Beth.'

'Takes one to know one.'

That evening, Beth and I go out with Jamie and Adam on our first proper dates. Beth and I make ourselves up as best we can, in the leisure centre loos with the make-up kits that her mum put together. We'd had one really long session with her on Wednesday night, when she showed us how to use different styles to suit the mood, or the different things we might be going to do. She even showed us how to be really over the top, just in case we were ever invited to something wacky. It's great, like having your own disguise outfit in your bag. I reckon she must have been a bit of a raver in her time, Beth's mum.

Despite all she said, Beth's wearing the clothes she bought at the charity shop, slightly altered by her auntie this afternoon and she looks cool in a sexy, quite grown-up sort of way. We go down to Maria's dad's place (Maria's a girl in our class), Pizza the Action, and although we have a laugh and stuff, I'm never quite sure I'm really getting through to Adam. I know I like him and all that, but for some reason I still don't want to leap on him, like I've heard you're supposed to.

My shy brother finally made his move on Beth on the way home on Saturday night and for the last couple of days I've hardly been able to get a word out of either of them. Beth, as far as I can make out, is in total, can't-think-about-anything-else, love-mode. Adam and I ended up outside my house and had a proper, tongues-and-hands everywhere snog-fest. Right at the end, however, when we come up for air, he tells me that his brother is still going on about me. I then tell him he's been round that afternoon.

'What do you really think of him, Ell?'

'Look, I don't want to be rude, Ad, but would you be offended if I said I think he's a bit of a sleaze-bag? I'm sure he was thinking of asking me out, but when he saw what I looked like after footie, he realised that I wasn't the babe he'd met at the ball. Anyway, what's he doing even thinking of asking me out knowing that you and I are . . .' I trail off, feeling embarrassed.

'But you *do* fancy him, don't you? Everyone else seems to.'

'I think he's lush to look at and all that, but I don't know anything about him. Anyway, I like you much more.'

'Really?'

'Really.'

Deep Thought for the Day

Snogging's dead weird. Half the time it seems fab and makes you feel all funny inside, but the rest of the time I can't really work out what I'm doing. I mean, how strange is it sticking your tongue in someone's mouth and vice versa? I keep wondering why I'm doing it when I'm doing it. Why do I even want to? I mean, you don't see animals snogging, do you? Or fish?

I get home at about nine-thirty and find Hannah watching telly in the lounge.

'Hi, Han, what are you doing *in?*'

'I was waiting for Greg to call, but he hasn't, as usual.'

Oh damn, I think. Do I tell her what happened or not? Suddenly I feel really sorry for my big sister and decide to go for it. Talk about head-in-lion's-mouth time.

'He came round to the leisure centre this afternoon.'

She whips round and sits bolt upright.

'What? What was he doing there?'

'He came to see me. Sorry.'

'You're joking!'

'I think he was a bit shocked to see me in football kit.'

'Did you talk to him?'

'For a bit. He didn't know what to say.'

'He must have said something!'

'He went on about how much he enjoyed meeting me last Saturday.'

'You're kidding. The rotten creep. Then what?'

'Look, I'm sorry, Hannah, but he was going to ask me out, till he actually saw me.'

'What do you mean?'

'He was expecting to meet someone like whoever he thought I was last Saturday.'

'I bet he bloody was.'

'I think he's a complete prat, Hannah.'

'I suppose I've known that since I first met him. He is ever so fit though, isn't he?'

'He's still a prat.'

Hannah suddenly looks like a little girl about to cry. I go over and put my arms round her.

'You can do better than him – we all can,' I say softly.

She suddenly lets go and sobs uncontrollably.

'Why do I think he's so wonderful, Ell?'

'He probably would be, if he wasn't so full of himself.'

'Flipping hell, Ell, I sometimes think you're more grown-up than me.'

'Look, I don't know anything, honest.'

'You know a slime-bag when you see one, which is more than I do.'

On Monday evening Beth phones me on the house phone.

'Guess what? I've just had a call from the *Rainsfield Gazette*. They want to do an interview with us. It's about those pictures they took. They know we're schoolgirls, thanks to big-gob Becks. Apparently she told them our proper names, how old we are and where we live. They went and got my number through directory enquiries. They think it's a good story. Everyone likes makeovers, the reporter said. I told them that I'd have to talk to you.'

'Hell's bells, Beth, we can't do it! Everyone'll take the piss. Anyway, what have we got to say? It's not exactly a story to shake the nation – *Teenage Girls Dress-Up Sensation!* – they must be desperate.'

'I know what you mean. But not when you see the crap they usually have. Anyway, what else can we do? I said I'd ring them back.'

'We could try telling the truth. That'd be original.'

'What's that? – I've forgotten.'

'Oh, you know, that the ball was a one-off and we only

said those daft names because we didn't want to be recognised.'

'Trouble is, I'm not so sure I don't want not to be recognised anymore. I think it could be a bit of a laugh – fame and all that. Think of what old Miss B would say.'

We talk for a bit and then Beth says, 'By the way, Hannah came over to ours last night to talk to Mum and Mum rang a few of the people she's kept up with over the years. You know, the ones who are still in the fashion business. One of the bosses of a model agency – called All Things Bright and Beautiful, I think she said – rang back today. She reckoned she could do some work experience through the Easter hols, if she wanted. Is Hannah there now?'

'Yeah, I'll go get her.'

I can hear Hannah talking all excited on the phone for a few minutes and then she bursts into my room.

'Ell, you'll never guess what! It looks like I've got an interview next week, with a model agency. It's all down to Beth's mum. It's only work experience, but it sounds like everything I've ever wanted. I'm going down to talk Mum and Dad.'

I listen at the top of the stairs, only to hear voices getting higher and higher and louder and louder. Mum seems to be laying down the law again big time, but eventually it quietens down and Hannah strolls out looking quite happy. She leaps up the stairs to talk to me.

'They don't mind me doing it, though you know Mum's worried that I'll get sucked in and won't bother with my A-levels and going to uni. Then I said maybe trying this will get it out of my system and that seemed to persuade her to let me do it.'

'Do you know what it involves?'

'I do, sort of. Beth's mum says I'll probably just be making the coffee and seeing that the models and photographers have everything they need. She said I might have to ring around to check their availability. How bad's that?'

'Where is it – the office?'

'In Chelsea apparently – just off the King's Road. Cool or what? I can go in on the bus. Honest, Ell, I can't believe it. Thanks, sweet.'

'What did I do? I only talked to Beth's mum.'

'Yeah, but you really didn't have to, especially after the way I've been with you lately.'

'Not just lately. You've always been a bit like that. Most of the time you've treated me as if I don't exist, or if I do, I'm not worth bothering about.'

'I didn't think that at all. I think you must have imagined it.'

'It seemed like that to me.'

'Oh, I don't know. Maybe I really was a bit jealous. It's just how you always seem to do everything right, and take things as they come. I'm always so hyper about everything. And I know you used to think me dumb for being into clothes and boys and stuff – but look at you now! You're the same as me!'

'How d'you make that out?'

'Well, you're into the same things.'

Not nearly as much as you, I say to myself.

'Anyway, I hope Greg will leave you alone now. I've told him you're under-age.'

'Oh, thanks,' I reply sarcastically.

'I suddenly felt almost protective towards you at that ball. Seeing you all lovely-looking and with blokes flocking round you like vultures, I realised that if you were anything like I was at your age, you could be in trouble. You might have looked all cool and grown-up on the outside, but on the inside you were still my little sister.'

'I'm not as dumb as you think, you know. I knew what they were after. But it was a bit weird, I admit.'

'You two really did look amazing – people are still talking about it. Especially Greg. It really annoyed me, at first.'

'You must have seen him since Saturday night?' I say.

Hannah looks sheepish for a moment.

'Yeah, it was actually *on* Saturday night. He rang me after I'd spoken to you, really late. I wanted to hate him, but I still went over to his place. I couldn't help it. He came to get me in his new car – it's a red Alfa Romeo. Then I stayed over. Don't tell Mum. I said I was at Louise's.'

'What do you mean, "stayed over"?' My mind races again. Hell! How could he do *that* to my sister just after he'd been chatting *me* up?

'I'm crazy about him, Ell. I know he's arrogant, and smooth and all that, but I can't help it – he's so good-looking and fun and cool. I sort of feel I'm lucky to be out with him, especially when there are so many girls who would kill to be in my shoes'

'But how does he feel about you?' I ask, trying to get my head round it.

'I think he likes me – and all the rest, of course. It's just that everything's on his terms and I let it be like that.'

'Maybe you should try making him work a bit harder.'

'I always mean to but whenever he rings, I just seem to do whatever he wants.'

Hannah and I talk on and on for what seems ages, probably longer than all the other times put together. I even get on to stuff I haven't been able to talk about with anyone except Beth: Adam, the boys at footie, wearing make-up, suddenly being attractive to guys – all that sort of thing. It's so brilliant. I've suddenly got a big sister I can talk to. I only hope it lasts.

Hannah's Surprise

Hannah comes home in a real state the following Wednesday after her visit to the model agency. She'd taken an afternoon off school – girl problems, I think she'd said. I've just got back from footie practice and she's bouncing up and down in the most alarming fashion.

Talking of fashion, the agency told her she could work there for the Easter holidays and then for the whole of the summer break, if Easter works out. Mum, bless her, sounds OK about it, which is pretty big of her after everything she said before. It turned out that all the agency had wanted Hannah to have, was a nice telephone voice and to be keen. She really looked nice. Instead of the stuff she usually wears, she had on a new white T-shirt, black jeans and a loose black linen jacket (borrowed from Mum), with medium-high black boots. Best of all, she'd asked me and Beth to help do her make-up and, instead of the over-the-top glossy stuff she usually plasters on, we made her look all soft and subtle for a change. It was amazing how much better she looked and more amazing when we realised how much we'd learned from Beth's mum.

A few weeks later, after we've broken up for Easter, Hannah comes home tired but happy after her first day. I can't wait to find out how it went.

'It was so wicked, Ell. I've got my own desk and my own

phone, and everyone talks to me like I'm a grown-up. It was so not like school.'

'Did you meet any models?'

'Millions – they pop in and out all the time. They're quite ordinary in real life, not glamorous at all. My boss, Suzie, is like their mum. One of the other girls in the office told me she looks after some of their money and only gives them it when they need it. It's so they won't blow it all on clothes, apparently. Oh yeah, and I met this really fit young photographer, Rory. He sat and talked with me for ages. Talk about cool. He had long blond hair in a pony-tail and, just as he was leaving, I looked out of the window and saw that he had a convertible Porsche – a 911 Targa – the one where the roof goes down before you actually get in.'

I can't help thinking how perfect the job is for my sis. Everything she's into – from glamour to blokes to flash cars to clothes – all rolled up into one.

Being my sister, she goes on and on and on and on, of course, until, just as she's about to go downstairs, she stops in her tracks.

'Oh, by the way, I almost forgot, I was showing one of the other girls the pictures of you and Beth and she took them to the boss.'

I try not to appear that interested, but I am. 'I didn't know you had them. Why did you want to show them?'

'Oh, I don't know. I suppose I thought you looked better than some of the models on the wall. Some of them are really ugly, I reckon.'

'I don't know whether that's a compliment or not.'

'You'll never guess what she said?' she went on, ignoring what I said.

'Who?'

'Suzie, my boss.'

'Don't tell me. She thought they were crap. Look, they were only taken by Beth's dad.'

'Calm down, Ell. Actually she said you both looked good. She wanted to know all about you both. I told her Beth was your best friend, and also who Beth's mum was. She said she hadn't seen Beth's mum for years and that she'd been one of the very best in the business. My boss used to be a model herself. She hadn't even known that her old friend had a husband let alone a daughter, until she rang her a few days ago. Anyway, then she said there's a real move to have curvy girls as well as slim ones. Normally, she didn't think Beth would have been tall enough to be a fashion model, but because she's so pretty, she'd probably get away with it, especially on the sort of work she's got in mind. Also Beth's colouring makes her more commercial. Anyway that's what Suzie said. Don't blame me.'

'So she wants to see us both?' I say rather stupidly. 'Me too?'

'I didn't see anyone else in the pictures, apart from the cat in the background. She said you made a good pair. She reckoned the contrast was interesting and that it really came across that you were mates. She might even get double bookings. She really thanked me for showing her the pictures.'

Without wanting to be ungrateful, I'm sure Hannah only showed her the pictures to suck up to her.

'I've got to ring Beth. I can't believe this,' I say.

We talk for a bit more and then I manage to get to the phone.

'Hi, Beth. It's me. I had to talk to you. Hannah's just got back from her first day at work.' I then tell her all about it, including the bit about our pictures and being models and stuff.

'Oh man, what are we going to tell the parents?' murmurs Beth.

'I tell you what, let's talk to your mum first. I've got a bit of thinking to do before I even mention it to mine.'

I decide at this point not to say that I'm not even sure I want to do it yet. It's so weird, I know I really wanted to hear what Hannah's boss thought, but now I have to start thinking of the reality of being an actual model. I keep remembering how I felt at the ball. Imagine how it would be if it was like that all the time. Imagine having to look good every time you go anywhere in public, with everyone judging you purely on how you look.

Beth's mum was very calm when we told her, almost like she'd already guessed. First of all, she went through to the other room, picked up the phone and rang her old friend Suzie who was still in her office. They talked for what seemed for ever, but I suppose that was because they hadn't met for yonks.

When she came back in the room she was smiling.

'Sorry, you two. We were just catching up a bit. Suzie's such a dear. She said she can't promise anything, but the timing is perfect – they're having a sort of spring clear out of models who aren't getting any work. It's a tough business you know. They certainly don't carry passengers. She asked if I'd like to come in with you, because she wants to talk to you both about what's involved and then, if she thinks you're suitable and if you want, you can have some proper test shots taken. She said it won't cost anything at this stage – the agency pays.'

I can't help wondering if the beautiful Rory, who Hannah had lusted over, would be taking our pictures.

'Anyway,' Beth's mum goes on, 'she said she has several really young girls on her books and that she keeps far more of an eye on them than the others. Now Beth, darling, are you sure you want to do this?'

Poor old Beth looks as if she's about to cry.

'Have you spoken to your parents, Ella?'

I know I should tell her what I've been thinking, but I don't.

'No fear. Not yet. I think they'll go straight through the roof. They want me to study and go to university and be clever and everything.'

'You still can. Would you like me to talk to your mum? We seem to understand each other pretty well, I think.'

'Would you?'

'I can't guarantee anything. Being a mum myself, I know how she must feel. It all looks pretty glamorous from the outside, but having been in the business once, I know both sides of it.'

It's weird, half of me's all sort of excited, and the other half feels like I'm being pushed into something that I've not really thought through.

The Great Inquisition

'Ella, could you come down here, please.'

It's Dad, and he's calling from the kitchen. When I get down, he's sitting at the table with Mum. They're both wearing their serious, determined-not-to-smile faces.

'We've had a phone call from Beth's mother,' Dad says.

I look down at the floor and suddenly feel like I've done something terribly, terribly wrong.

'I believe you might know what it's about.'

I nod slowly, fairly sure where this is going. Mum takes over. She smiles weakly.

'To tell you the truth, darling,' she says all softly, 'we don't know whether to be upset or happy for you.'

I shift from foot to foot, realising that it's not my turn to speak.

'Neither of us has had anything to do with that particular world, but what you hear about it sometimes sounds pretty ghastly.'

I so want to tell them that I'm far from into it myself, but decide to leave my grand entry just a little bit longer.

'All this is as much of a shock to us as it must be to you. When we saw you all dressed up we couldn't believe it actually *was* you. You do realise that you're only going to have your photographs taken to see if they want to take you on their books. Beth's mother told me she doesn't want your hopes built up too much. She said they see hundreds of girls and most just don't really work in front of the camera.'

'Anyway, darling, your father and I have discussed it for the best part of an hour now and have decided that if you want to do it, we won't stand in your way. We realise that for most young girls it's just a dream. I'll be honest, Ella darling, I was all for stopping it before it started, but your father believes that if we were to try, you might hate us for it.'

My turn.

'Look, Mum, I'm not that sure that I want to do it either, to be dead honest. Beth is, big time, but I'm not. It's just that Gran always says that you should try everything before having an opinion. Another thing Gran always said is that you're a long time grown-up, and that you should take all the chances that come along.'

Mum turns to Dad with a big grin on her face.

'Trust your mother to say the right thing at the wrong time.'

'Well,' says Dad, suddenly standing up with a big smile on his face too, 'I don't know about you two, but I think this calls for a little celebration. Would you like a glass of wine, Ella darling? We might as well toast your growing up'

Dad pours me out a glass (for the first time ever) and then holds his own up and does a sort of funny speech thing.

'To my beautiful, growing-up daughter.'

Deep Thought for the Day

I don't think that parents really have any more clue of what they want for their kids than they do for themselves. I just think they're so scared sometimes about anything that even looks as if it might be risky, that they would rather they went in for a dull job, because at least it will be safe.

Just then, Jamie strolls in and sees me with a drink in my hand.

'Jeez, what's going on here? Is that Ribena or has Dad won the lottery?'

'You'd better tell him, Ell darling,' says Mum.

I explain to my brother what's happened. Mum and Dad don't really know that Beth's his girlfriend now and can't understand why he looks so worried.

'I just hope you two won't go all snotty, that's all.'

'How do you mean?'

'Oh you know, thinking you're better than the rest of us, like.'

'Why should we do that?'

'Whenever you see people like supermodels interviewed on telly, they seem so up their own . . . er . . . well, you know where – like they think they're the dog's boll – '

I jump in.

'I'm only going for some test shots, for God's sake.'

'Yeah, but you could be up there one day. Stranger things have happened.'

'Oh, come on! Look, they'll probably take one look at us and say thanks but no thanks.'

I decided to go ahead with it, at least so that I could hear what the woman at the model agency would say. It's now Friday and the last day of the Easter holidays. We are getting ready to leave for the agency and Beth's mum says that we should keep our make-up to a minimum. They prefer to see you looking as natural as possible. She tells us that there'll probably be a photographer in the office with a digital camera to take reference pictures. That's the way it usually works – only they were Polaroids in her day. I decide to wear my new (second-hand) brown suede mini-skirt with a black, long-sleeve figure-hugging jumper, and a pair of black tights with matching trainers (which were white until Mum helped me dye them). Mum lends me her favourite Indian silver and turquoise necklace to set the whole thing off.

Beth chooses a long black skirt, with a fairly low-cut black silk blouse (borrowed from *her* mum) and the black Spanish-style boots she got for Christmas. Her mum then quickly does our hair just before setting off in the car for Chelsea.

'Are you nervous?' Beth asks me when we're in the back of the car.

'Sort of. But not as much as I thought I would be. I looked a bit of a beast when I got up this morning, like I'd been beaten by the ugly stick.'

'You idiot. You look great. I can't wait.'

'I just wish I could have the full paint job,' I moan. 'You're all right, you don't need it.'

When we get to the office, in a side street halfway up the King's Road, Hannah runs out all excited from the back room and leads us proudly through the main office to show us her desk and chair and phone and coffee cup and stuff. She's even got her favourite little teddy bear sitting to one side (how stupendously and monumentally naff is that on a scale of one to a million?). Beth's mum then does this whole lovey-lovey, kissy-kissy, you-haven't-changed-a-bit routine with this Suzie woman. Apparently, they really haven't seen each other for over fifteen years. Suzie seems quite nice, but not someone you'd ever want *not* to be on your side, we decided after. On the way here, Beth's mum had said she was one of the best and toughest in the business. You can tell Suzie was once a model herself, just by the way she moves about. In another room, I can just make out a little studio set-up with lights and a long sweep of what looks like white paper running down the back and on to the floor.

'Jeez, Ell, this is all a bit proper,' whispers Beth.

'Are we going to have to pose and stuff?' I ask.

'Don't know. Best just to wait for someone to tell us what to do.'

Suzie comes over to talk to us.

'Hello darlings, thank you so much for coming all this way. I must say you both look really scrumptious. Ben's just going to take a few mug shots to start with for our books. We'll see how that goes and then Ben will set up some lighting so that we can take a few more that will hopefully be good enough to show prospective clients. If you could put a little more make-up on Ella, Sandra darling, that would help. She's looking a little too healthy even for us. Beth doesn't really need anything, but we might do something a bit more dramatic with her eyes to pull them out more. Know what I mean, darling?'

After he's taken the snaps with the digital camera, Ben the photographer (simply divine, according to Hannah later) loads them on to the computer, and shows Suzie. She then tells him exactly what she's after. The whole thing seems to take for ever and by the time he's ready, I'm nearly walking up the wall with boredom.

'Righto, sweetie,' the photographer calls. 'Ella, isn't it? If we could just have you standing sideways to me and just turning your head a little this way and down slightly. That's absolutely fabulous, darling. Now push your hips forward – that's the way – and keep your legs and feet together so you're making a simple curved line like a bow. That's perfect, sweetie. Now, if you could point your left hand and arm in the direction you're facing? Beautiful – you're an absolute natural.'

After he's done about a million of these, he does the same sort of thing with Beth, only with her, he starts with her sitting down with her knees apart and her chin resting on her hands. He then gets me to stand right behind her and put my arms round her.

Then it happens! Just as I'm about to lose my balance, I accidentally grab hold of Beth's left boob, thinking it's her elbow, and she lets out a little giggly squeal. I realise what I've done and start to giggle too. This is all Beth and me have ever needed to lose the plot completely. Before very long, we're both falling about in fits of terminal laughter like only we can. Oddly enough, the photographer keeps snapping away and even starts laughing himself. Suzie and Beth's mum have been standing at the back ready to study the images when they come up on the computer screen. I know we must have blown it, and am ready to be sent home, but after a short while, Suzie tells Ben that she has enough to work with. It turns out that she loved the ones with me and Beth giggling because they showed off our 'natural youthfulness', whatever that means.

'You girls look so at ease in front of the camera. I can't see how any of my clients will be able to resist. I have someone to send these to right away. Well done, girls.'

Well done for what? I think. All we did was stand in front of a flipping camera and lark about. Surely people don't pay people for that . . . or do they?

That photo shoot has got me in a worse state than I was before. Apart from the end bit, with Beth, I was *so* bored. Beth, of course, is over the moon. The model's life's the only one for her, she says, and she jabbers away to her mum all the way home . . . it must run in her family. It turns out even her mum's mum – her granny – was in the fashion business back in the olden days. Mind you, my own gran was a model for a bit too. Anyway, so as not to be a wet blanket, I make all the right noises at the right times, being as keen as I can be when asked what I think of Suzie, the office, the photographer and all that. But, underneath, I get this sneaking feeling that they might have sussed that it's not for me. On top of all that, neither of us know how to break it to the girls at school or what their reaction will be when we do.

Facing the Class

It's Monday morning, the first day of the new term, and Beth and I have just arrived in our classroom. We'd decided that we'd tell no one where we'd been on Friday, but as soon as we're through the door, it's obvious they all know. Suddenly everyone strikes an exaggerated pose, like they'd been rehearsing. Then Becky Swithin strides down the centre aisle, dropping her blazer off her shoulders, fluttering her eyelids and swinging her hips like crazy – followed by Emma and Donna.

'OK, who told on us?' I ask.

'Golly gosh, they're still speaking to us,' Emma blurts out, 'we are *so* honoured.'

'Shut it,' yells Beth. 'How did you find out?'

'We just bought a copy of *Vogue*, of course. You look simply divine, darling.'

Beth and I wait for the cackling to die down and try again.

Tilly looks straight at me.

'Your boyfriend told Craig at football on Saturday. He's a mate of my brother's and he told me.'

The girls carry on taking the piss for another five minutes or so, but after a while they can't resist asking what it was really like. Just as we're getting into it, Miss Braithwaite comes striding through the door. She clocks straight away that the girls are gathered round Beth and me.

'All right, you two, what have you been up to now?'

'Nothing, Miss,' says Beth nervously.

The rest of the girls start tittering. I can see straight away where this is going.

'This hasn't got anything to do with your alter egos, has it?'

Beth and I look at each other blankly, but although we don't understand what she said, we know full well what she's getting at.

'Ellesandra and Bethany, if I remember rightly,' she persists. 'That's who you are when you're not being you. Isn't that right?'

'Yes, Miss,' I say sheepishly.

'How are the dear girls?' she continues sarcastically.

'They're models now, Miss,' Becky blurts out. I could murder her and probably will sometime.

'Models, eh? Well, well, well. Come on then, tell us all about it, Ella.'

'There's nothing to tell Miss. Beth and I just went along for some test shots, that's all.'

'So this is what we've been attempting to educate you for, is it?'

'What, Miss?'

'To stand in front of a camera, flaunting your bodies.'

'We weren't nude,' Beth says almost crossly.

'It doesn't take much brainpower though, does it?'

We both look at the ground, hoping that she'll stop if we don't say anything. Suddenly Donna McAllister, the class genius, pipes up.

'Why does everything worthwhile have to involve our brains, Miss? Loads of people do things that don't involve deep thinking – like athletes and dancers and all the people who do physical work.'

Miss Braithwaite looks positively shocked at this outburst. Her mouth falls open and she struggles for words.

'I-I'm surprised to hear that coming from you, Donna. I'd have thought that, like me, you'd have thought merely standing in front of a camera was a pretty worthless occupation.'

'It's not something you do for the rest of your life, Miss. I think Ella and Beth are jolly lucky to get the chance.'

At this point a small cheer goes round the rest of the girls.

'I don't know why I bother,' says Miss Braithwaite, looking really miffed, 'I might as well start up a modelling school.'

We all look at our teacher and then at each other. Suddenly the whole class bursts into fits of laughter.

All Confused and Talking to Mum

That night, I decide to talk to my mum while she's doing supper.

'This modelling business. I don't know why, but I'm certain something's going to happen soon, and I'm not sure I want it to.'

Mum pours herself a glass of wine and sits down at the kitchen table.

'I can't say I'm heartbroken, darling – that would be lying, but why in particular?'

'I suppose it's because I'm having such a good time without it. I love doing football and all the other stuff. I even quite like school at the moment. I just reckon life will all change. I don't really feel ready for that.'

'Couldn't you do with some extra money?'

'Of course – but I'm not that desperate. Maybe it's something I can do later.'

'I thought you really enjoyed getting all dressed up. Some people even thought you *were* a model, according to Hannah.'

'I did, Mum, but it wasn't really me. It was like a fancy dress sort of thing.'

'What are you going to tell Beth?'

'That's what I'm really worried about, yeah. She'll hate me. Especially if it mucks up her chances.'

'It's much better to tell her now rather than later. I've

already talked quite a bit to her mother. She's twigged you're not nearly so keen as Beth. She's a bright lady, that one.'

'And then there's Hannah,' I say.

'What about Hannah?'

'Well, she got me into the whole thing at that agency, even if it was by accident. She might go off her rocker if I back out.'

'I'm afraid that's her problem. She can't blame you if you feel it's not really what you want. Anyway, it was down to you and Beth that she was there in the first place.'

'It's a real drag – it's about the first time we've ever really got on.'

'I'm amazed that I can have two children so different. Poor Hannah would die to have a chance to be a model. Look, knowing Hannah, she might secretly be relieved that she's not going to have to watch her sister getting all that attention.'

'You might be right. It's just that I'd feel a bit like I was rubbing her nose in it if I turned it down. Know what I mean?'

'Don't you be so silly. It's your life and who knows, you could change your mind again later on. The future's a long time. And anyway, you might well not get hired even if you were a model.'

Adam and I are turning out to be a bit of an item. Everyone seems to know about it at school and the other guys in the footie team have started making sarky comments. I do like him lots, but although the other girls say they think he's well

158

fit, I just can't seem to get that worked up. Trouble is, I'm not sure I could ever get that worked up about anyone. My mates seem to eat, drink and breathe the male of the species, going on and on for what seems like for ever. As if whoever's listening is remotely interested, I say.

Deep Thought for the Day

I've noticed that most of my friends just talk and hardly ever listen. Even when they're not talking, it's as if they're busy trying to think of what they're going to say when they can get in next. I mentioned it to my brother and he says it's called 'all transmit and no receive'. Whatever it's called, it's bloody annoying. Thank God Beth's not like that.

I've been snogging Adam for a few weeks now and I suppose it's own-up time.

Here goes – the whole truth and nothing but the truth! I have to say, if I was strapped down and tortured to within an inch of my life, that, from the not-being-able-to-sleep-till-I-snogged-him-properly stage (after the back of the car), I'm getting a bit bored. It's got me thinking about the whole sex thing. Everyone goes on and on about it, but I'm beginning to wonder if people only do proper sex just to relieve the monotony of the first bit – like it's something different. I mean, sex seems like an odd thing anyway if you think about what actually goes on (and what goes where!). Apart from all that, I've seen enough movies and soaps to realise that married couples seem to have problems with it – even if they love each other! Mum and Dad are probably bored with it too, so what hope have I got? I'm bored already and I haven't even done it yet!

One night, walking home with Beth after gym, we get to talking about *it*. It's funny, but since she's been seeing Jamie, we've hardly mentioned boys or any related subjects – especially sex. I suppose, if truth be known, I'd really rather not know what my brother and my best friend get up to when I'm not there.

'Has Jamie asked you much about modelling?' she asks, completely out of the blue.

'Bits and pieces, but nothing much. He did say, right at the beginning, before we'd even been to see that agent woman, that he hoped we didn't get all "snotty" – I think he said.'

'He's weird about it with me. He keeps telling me he sort of likes me the way I am, and that he doesn't really go for the all glammed-up look. He says it changes me, like I'm different and stuff. He says I even talk funny.'

'He might have a point. Do you remember what we were like at the ball, all sort of pretend posh?'

'Yeah, but we were only messing about,' says Beth.

'You say that, but who else have we met recently who went on like that all the time?'

Beth walks on for a bit and then stops dead.

'You don't mean? Not that Suzie woman at the model agency?'

'You bet I do. It was all that *darling* this and *sweetie* that, just like those women in *Absolutely Fabulous*. You know . . . Patsy and Eddie.'

'Yeah, but when we do it, we're so seriously not serious.'

'My gran once told me not to cross my eyes too much for a joke or stick my tongue out, in case the wind changed and I got stuck like it.'

'What d'you mean?'

'It's a bit like Miss Braithwaite. She's got so used to talking in that clever Dick, ever-so-slightly-sneery way, that I bet she can't do any different now. I'm not sure, but maybe Jamie thinks we'll talk like that if we start dressing up all the time and going to smart places.'

'I never thought of that.'

'It obviously matters a lot what my brother thinks, Beth.'

'I know. I haven't talked about him much – cos he's your brother and it's a bit difficult, but I really do like him, Ell. He's lush. I think I more than like him. Like I think I might actually I –'

'Stop there, Beth! Don't mention the L-word, for God's sake.'

'Sorry, but I can't talk to anyone about it, not even you, because he's your flipping brother. It's driving me bonkers, Ell. I try to talk to Mum a bit, but it's not the same. I'm crazy about him – I always have been, but I keep thinking he'll get fed up with me and find someone else.'

'Jamie's not like that. He takes a long time to get going – you should know that – but when he does find something, or someone, he likes, he tends to stay with it. Anyway, he'd never dare do the dirty on you. He knows I'd cut his willy off.'

'Jeez, don't do that, Ell. Not yet anyway!'

'BETH! Go and wash your mouth out! How dare you have such thoughts about my brother?'

161

'I haven't asked you about Adam for ages.'

'I sort of wish I felt like you do about Jamie. I like him and all that, but if I'm honest, I'm getting a bit bored. We never really talk about anything, just snog. Tell the truth, I suppose I'd rather be out with you most of the time. Does that sound a bit weird?'

'I know what you mean. Boys do get in the way of mates sometimes. If I really think about it, I have more to talk about with you than Jamie.'

We walk along deep in thought for a while and then I decide that the time is as good as it's ever going to be to come out with what else is on my mind.

'Beth, look, I've got something else to say, but I'm not sure how you're going to take it. Feel free to kill me if you have to.'

Beth knows me so well. She realises it's going to be important and slows down and stares right into my eyes.

'It's about this modelling thing isn't it?' she says quietly. 'You haven't talked about it for ages. Only when I bring it up.'

'I know. I'm sorry. I don't quite know how to say this. It's just that I'm not sure I want to go on with it.'

'How do you mean?'

'Oh, Beth, I just don't think it's for me. I've been worrying about it ever since we did those tests.'

'But it was a laugh, wasn't it? Don't you remember when we were falling about giggling?'

'I think that was because it was all new. I bet it would get boring after a while.'

'What would you rather be doing?'

'In a way, what I'm doing now. Playing footie, and going to school and all that. It doesn't really fit in with modelling.'

'Why not?'

'Oh, you know. I'm always getting scuffs and bruises when I'm playing. I'd have to stop all that. Unless I got a job modelling for Elastoplast.'

'But we were going to be a team,' Beth says, ignoring my pathetic joke.

'I know, and I'm really sorry, honest, but I think it's better to tell you now than later.'

'But I've gone to all that trouble to get slim and fit. Now it's all bloody wasted.'

'It's not, Beth. That's stupid. Look, Suzie said we looked great together – but that didn't mean we didn't look great apart. Anyway, I bet there'll be stuff for you to do by yourself. Especially for beauty products.'

'Are you going to tell them at All Things Bright and Beautiful?'

'Yeah, I already talked with Mum last night. I was going to wait to see if we were offered work, but she reckoned they'd be less annoyed if I told them now. She's going to phone your mum after I've spoken to you.'

'Are you sure?'

'I think I am . . . sorry.'

Crap friend alert. I don't think I've ever done anything as difficult as that. Poor Beth looks like I've completely destroyed her life.

Strange Men in My Goal

It's Saturday afternoon and we're playing South Beckington Juniors at home. We usually don't get that many spectators, especially if the team we're up against isn't much good, but all through the first half, I can't help noticing this strange bloke. He's about my dad's age, with a bald head, a big moustache and a long raincoat and he's standing right by the left-hand goalpost watching me like our cat watches the bird table. By half-time we're two-nil up and really giving the other team a good seeing to. Without showing off, I've played my part pretty well, warding off three or four shots and a penalty. (To be completely honest, the guy who took it missed by miles.)

When it comes to the second half, this guy in the raincoat moves up to the other end with me and carries on watching till the final whistle. If this is stalking, I think, he's pretty crap at it. All the same, I don't like it one bit and begin to get nervous. Anyway, we win the game five-nil, and when it's over, he strolls across and stands right in front of me with a big smile on his face. I half expect him to open his raincoat to show me his credentials. Beth and I had one like that in our park once but he ran away when Beth pointed and giggled.

'Well played,' he says. 'You've probably noticed I've been watching you.'

I nod suspiciously. At first I think he just wants to be

friendly, but even so, I look around nervously for my mates. Luckily a few of them have also clocked him and are beginning to gather round.

'I'm Tom Gillespie,' he continues, 'the manager of Rainsfield Ladies first team. You've probably heard of us — we've just been promoted to the premier division this year. I reckon we're one of the best teams around, though I say it myself. Our keeper, Jenny Bickerstaff, is leaving next season to have a baby and it's my job to find a replacement. We normally choose from our B or C teams, but someone just happened to mention that they'd seen you a couple of times and said that I should come down and take a look — especially as you live in Rainsfield. I must admit, from seeing you play today, I'm rather impressed.'

'Aren't I a bit too young to be in the proper league?' I ask.

'Our lower age limit is fourteen. I've done my homework, you see. I wondered if you'd like to come to a trial work-out next week. Look — Ella, isn't it? — I'll be completely straight with you, we have two other possibilities, so we thought we'd get you all together. That's if you're interested?'

I head back towards the showers in a bit of a daze. Rainsfield Ladies football team are quite famous in our area. They do far better than the equivalent mens clubs and this year gave everyone a real shock when they reached the premier league. Mind you, for me the timing's a bit spooky. Just as I've decided not to go on with the modelling thing, this shows up. Is it a sign from above?

When I get inside, the rest of the team gather round and examine the card he left.

'Are you leaving us, Ell?' asks Adam, sadly.

'I don't know. I haven't even thought about it. Look, they haven't even picked me yet,' I reply, 'and I haven't even decided if I want to play in an all-girls team anyway.'

I have really, but I'm hardly going to tell them that. At least if I do leave, it won't be because of the way the boys treated me when they discovered I was a girl. Thank God that's all in the past.

After we've showered, Adam catches up with me in the corridor.

'I've just heard you're not going ahead with the modelling thing.'

'Who told you that – Beth?'

'Well, Beth told Jamie and he told me. She was a bit annoyed, but you probably know that.'

'I don't really blame her, we went into it together – just for a laugh really, but I felt all funny about it.'

'Didn't you like it when you went for those tests?'

'I don't know really. It was weird. I just felt sort of fake – like it wasn't me they were photographing, but just who they had decided I was. Can you understand?'

'I suppose that's what the word "model" means.'

'Yeah, like I'm a model of something that I'm not. I was thinking about it the other day, when I was looking through a fashion magazine. All those beautiful girls, especially the young ones, look so sorted and sophisticated, but are probably just ordinary like me.'

'So the whole thing's a hype, you think. Is that a problem?'

'I suppose not, but I just didn't want it. For instance, I

couldn't carry on playing footie, I'd have to be really careful what I eat – I think I'm just too young for all that.'

'A lot of girls will think you're bonkers, choosing football instead of modelling.'

'A lot of girls think I'm bonkers anyway.'

'I think you're very brave.'

I stare at him for a second, and without even thinking about it, give him a great big sloppy kiss. Probably the first one I've really meant for a while.

The next great hurdle is to tell Hannah about my decision. I must admit I'm dreading it, especially as we've been getting on really well lately. I catch her just as she comes in and give it to her straight.

'Are you stark, staring mad?' she yells, throwing her bag on to her bed. 'I'd give anything to be in your shoes and you just throw it away.'

'It isn't as if I haven't thought about it, Hannah. It's been really worrying me.'

'There's nothing to bloody think about,' she rants on. 'Anyway, what about all the trouble I went to getting you the gig. I tell you, our agency's one of the best.

'I didn't actually ask you to do it in the first place, if you remember.'

'So you'd rather play your stupid football than stand a chance of being a top model?'

'I'm sorry, but at the moment I sort of would. I just don't feel ready for anything like that.'

'You're a funny girl, Ell. You've got it right at your feet and then you stick two fingers up.'

'There's always Beth. She wants to go ahead.'

'Just as well. There's a chance of a job for her for a new shampoo especially for her sort of hair – thick and wavy.'

'Have you told her yet?'

'No, we were waiting for confirmation. We don't want to build her hopes up. There might be quite a lot of money in it, especially if it gets on telly.'

For a split second . . .

Deep Thought for the Day

People are funny. They can become uninterested in something to the point of ignoring it completely, but if anyone they know shows any interest, they want it back. Children are like it with toys and dogs are like it with bones.

'You know you can always change your mind, don't you, Ell?' Hannah continues. 'Suzie was quite sad when you decided not to go ahead, but she thought you showed real balls to do it. She made me promise to ask you to keep in touch. It's amazing. She tries to avoid most of the girls who come in. It was usually my job to speak to them.'

'Is it as good as you thought?'

'It's better! I just love it! I wish I didn't have to go back to that poxy school, to be treated like a kid again. I feel when I'm at the agency that I'm on to the next bit of my life. And it's not just that, Ell. I think I'm actually really good at it. It's the first time I've been really good at anything, I suppose. Suzie said there might be a permanent job going and that she'd offer it to me. I told her Mum and Dad would never let me leave school, so she suggested meeting them and talking about it. I think she really likes me. The other day, she asked my opinion on what I thought of a couple of girls that came in for an interview, like the one you and Beth had.'

'How did that go?'

'It was a bit weird, really. I ended up feeling sorry for them. They wanted it so much, and I found myself being in a position to decide their whole future. Well, sort of.'

'That's what I was worried about in the first place,' I say. 'Imagine just relying on your looks to make a living. What if you get a huge spot on the end of your nose, or big bags under your eyes, like everyone does sometimes.'

'Don't talk about it, we had to send a girl home the other day. She'd obviously been at the drinks the night before. She was supposed to be doing a shoot for one of those sparkly mineral waters – all health and good living and stuff and she looked like the before shot in an ad for a hangover cure.'

'I bet Suzie went mad, didn't she?'

'She almost fired her on the spot and the poor girl lost it completely. I managed to talk her out of it.'

'Hey,' I say, 'have you heard? I'm going for a trial for the Rainsfield Ladies.'

'They're supposed to be quite good, aren't they?'

'They're in the premier league.'

'I suppose I ought to say well done, but heaven knows why. I'd hate to get all cold and dirty every week.'

'And I couldn't bear having to put on all that make-up and stuff every day.'

Out of the blue, Hannah looks at me all sort of soppy-like,

and then walks over and gives me a great big hug, the first I can ever remember.

'I've got something else to tell you, Ell. One of the male models at work asked me out next week. He's dead gorgeous and he really likes me. And guess what? There's better. Greg phoned me the other evening and more or less told me to come over. When I said no, he went all shirty, so I told him exactly what I thought of him. Can you believe it?'

I think I almost can. 'Well done, Hannah,' I say. Things are certainly looking up. You never know, I think I might even like having a big sister.

The Very Last Deep Thought for the Day

It's funny, you think you know someone really well, and then suddenly they do something that makes you think that everything you ever thought about them before, might be completely wrong. If I'm not very careful, my horrible sister Hannah might turn into a real mate.

If you would like more information about books
available from Piccadilly Press and how to order them,
please contact us at:

Piccadilly Press Ltd.
5 Castle Road
London
NW1 8PR

Tel: 020 7267 4492
Fax: 020 7267 4493

Feel free to visit our website at
www.piccadillypress.co.uk